It's an Ill-wind Indeed…

John K. Sutherland.

March 2021

The weather was absolute hell when they'd met on the top of the Fell, miles from anywhere.

The downpour had caught her totally off guard and she was soaking wet when he saw her, sheltering in the lea of a large clump of rocks.
He couldn't just ignore her, so he didn't.
'If he ignored her…?' no one should ignore another in distress out here.

She could refuse his help, but she didn't.

He sat down with her and unsnapped his poncho to include her under it with him, until the storm passed.

He should try and get her dry, or she'd never be able to go anywhere.

Nothing is ever as simple as it at first seems, as James soon discovered. There was something about her…!

He soon found out was that 'something' was. She didn't have a shy bone in her body and she was eager for his help.

The situation very quickly got out of control.

Table of Contents.

An unexpected encounter.

Rolling things along.

A misplaced sense of humor.

Tell me a little about yourself, James.

Learning even more about him.

Progression.

Could this be happening to us so soon?

Success!

No stuffing that Genie back into the bottle.

I would like to know more.

We need to leave here.

Home.

When the Cat's away…

Not a moment too soon.

An explosive confession.

Wrapping things up.

Knowing when to Accept the Inevitable.

Fait Accompli.

An unexpected encounter.

James was ready to head back to the Inn when the weather changed again.

The heavens opened.

He'd had some warning, seeing the wind pick up and the clouds moving in fast, along with thunder. He was on an exposed fell and standing on a 'basic' rock; a gabbro, a magnet for lightning. He'd better get to a lower elevation to avoid being struck by it.

He could see the rain front coming at him almost horizontally, but with too little warning, so had quickly unpacked his yellow slicker, a poncho style of covering designed for cyclists and horse riders, with loops inside, to attach it to his belt, and with other loops for his thumbs to hold it down on him, and to stop the wind taking it off him like a parachute. He concentrated on getting off the fell by the shortest route as the lightning flashed around him.

He counted; one... two... *'Boom'!*

It was too close. He picked up his pace.

But he wasn't alone.

Another one, not as well outfitted as he was, was sheltering in the lee of a large set of boulders at the edge of an outcrop. She was a young woman, and not dressed for this weather. What the hell was she doing out on these fells alone? She might get injured and then where would she be?

Who was he, to criticize her? He, was alone.

She was as shocked to see him as he was to see her. Maybe she was concerned about her safety with her being alone out here. However, he couldn't ignore her; not in this storm. She needed his help whether she wanted it or not, and he was obliged to give it, or at least, try.

She was miserable, drenched; with water running off her face. She was well enough dressed for cold weather--apart from the shorts-- but not for this unexpected downpour.

Her heavy sweater had protected her for a while, but it was as sodden as it could be, along with her shorts, and her legs were wet below them. She was sitting with her legs pulled up to her buttocks, and she was shivering, covered partially by a denim jacket as she hunkered down, away from the worst of it.

If she didn't get off the fell soon, her circumstance could rapidly become more dire, especially if it turned to snow, as it threatened to do. He'd have to help her with that.

He couldn't ignore her, and she was too damned wet for her own good, but how was he to help her without scaring the wits out of her, and her rebelling? He was damp himself in just the short time he'd struggled with things when the downpour had begun, but at least he could help her to survive this… if she would let him help her.

He'd need to be very careful. Whatever he suggested would be awkward, but he couldn't leave her like this, and wouldn't, unless she totally resisted him, and maybe not even then. It would be a tricky situation, and it would need some delicacy on his part.

She might just tell him to 'get lost'. Some young women were like that on principle.

He knelt in front of her, blocking some of the wind and driving rain, and smiled, looking down at her, hoping he wouldn't scare her.

"Hi."

She looked up at him as she blew water off the end of her nose. He hadn't needed to be so concerned about his reception. She didn't seem too shy, or too miserable, or even scared by him coming so close, but another ten minutes in this rain and the misery would get much worse, fast.

She was a good two hours away from getting down to where there was life of any kind that could help her. People had died of exposure for less than this, but he'd keep that thought to himself. She was lucky he'd seen her.

"I guess we both got caught by this."

She nodded, sending a cascade of water off her hair. She looked unhappy, but she was able to respond.

"I didn't expect this. The forecast was wrong. Again. It had this rain for yesterday, and it didn't come." She was wary of him, but not scared.

He commiserated. "The weather can't always be predicted up here."

This hadn't, that was sure. It had come down so hard that visibility had been down to a few yards and he'd got damp himself in just the minute it had taken him to get out of his backpack, unroll his slicker and get it on over everything; fighting with it to stop it being ripped out of his hands by the wind. There was room under if for his backpack too, so that was a good thing about it.

"I'm sorry for approaching you like this… out of the blue. If you will let me, I can help you."

Why was he apologizing for wanting to help her? She needed help, and she *had* been relieved to see him.

She looked at him more closely, looking up at him as he tried to explain.

She reminded him of his younger sister, but she wasn't his sister and he couldn't just barge in… guns blazing.

How much he could help, depended very much on her and how far she would let him go to get her warm, if not entirely dry. He didn't want to seem any more threatening to her than he already must seem.

"I'm dry and well enough protected under this. There is room for two to rest under here and get dry, with a few adjustments, for as long as it takes to get you warm, if that wouldn't scare you."

'With a few adjustments.'

'Scare her?'

She didn't look scared.

He tried to explain. "It will be close-quarters for a while. You need to get warmer than you are, and drier too." That much was obvious to anyone, especially and even, to her. He was offering to share his warmth with her. That suggestion seemed much better, than the way it was for her at this particular moment.

She almost didn't care what he did if it would protect her from getting any more wet, and cold, and especially if it would get her warm.

He waited for her to agree. It was the rest of it that would concern her; the part he wasn't telling her, but they'd have to negotiate that, once he'd got the ball rolling. She wasn't objecting. Not yet.

He took her silence as acquiescence.

There was no point in waiting for her to say anything. She wouldn't object so much now.

He shrugged out of his backpack, laid it beside her on the wet ground and sat on it before it also got wet, after taking a pack out of the top of it. He unsnapped a few things, and then lifted his poncho over her to include her under it as far as possible, pulling her closer into him as he unsnapped other things to open it up even more. They were both, mostly under it now.

He turned to her, placing one bent leg behind her, then—his heart beating, and ready to apologize—he lifted her easily; his hand under her bare legs, the other around her, and pulled her to sit high on his legs and to lean into him as he straightened his legs out to extend beyond the cover of the poncho, pulling it down around them.

He wasn't going to ask her permission for everything. That would have been stupid, as well as a waste of time.

He sensed that she was looking up at him from just a few inches away, seeing his hesitation and shyness in dealing with her.

He was strong, to have picked her up as easily as that. At least she was now out of the rain. She'd never seen this kind of protection against the weather before, but she'd heard of it.

He pulled the hood to cover the hole where his head had been, and rearranged the cover around them both, unfastening a few more snaps to make it larger, almost doubling its size as he pulled it down around them. He continued, adjusting everything so that it wouldn't blow away; holding it down with some loose rocks from where they were sitting, and even using his feet, as well as trapping it against the rock behind them with his body.

It was a coat that turned into a tent!

She almost laughed at that thought, except she was too miserable to laugh.

It was long enough and capacious enough to cover them both now, with not much room to spare. It would protect them from the rain and wind for long enough. They'd have to get down to the road before dark, but that was a good few hours away.

She had her eyes closed now, leaning against him, waiting to see how he would help her, and able to guess some of it. If she needed to object, she would.

She didn't say anything, but she did know something about him. She'd seen him on the fell before, at a distance. He was staying at the local Inn.

He hesitated for a while, then pulled her closer to him. She didn't resist. He tried to explain, shyly, not sure how to persuade her of what he would need to do.

"I'm sorry about this, but we don't have much choice, and there is little enough time before I'll need to get you down from here."

What was he apologizing for? He should just get on with it.

"I'll do my best to get you off this fell, before dark, but I can't carry you, so we'll have to get you warmer and drier first. We do have time for that. I'll help you as much as I can."

She was listening.

"First, we have to get you out of some of these wet clothes and get you warm. If you won't object too much."

Of course she would object, but he'd still have to do it.

He sounded cautious, and shy, not sure how she would respond to that statement.

She nodded, not objecting; seeming to give permission and to agree… to 'some' of it. At least she didn't argue, or physically resist what he was suggesting. She was too wet and cold for that.

It was tight quarters where they were, and would soon get more personal, but she'd survive. He would apologize where he needed to as he explained what he needed to do, and why. As embarrassing as it might be, it would beat getting any wetter, except she was now getting him wet where she leaned against him.

Despite that, she could feel his warmth.

As she got a little warmer, he thought about what he needed to do, and how he would have to explain it to her.

One step at a time, boy. Until she objected and stopped him.

Step one. He sighed.

"Your denim jacket and sweater are totally wet and are robbing your body of warmth. If you will let me…?"

He was asking before he did anything, waiting for her approval.

He went up a few more notches in her estimation of him as she looked at him. He had a concerned expression for her in his eyes and he was painfully shy… worried about how she would respond.

She had never seen him this close. Her first impression of him at a distance had been wrong. She relaxed more, into him. Whatever he needed to do to help her—within reason—she would not object to.

She nodded in response to his request. He was making sense, so far.

He was relieved to see that.

Rolling things along.

He lifted her jacket from her and watched as she made a start on getting rid of her sweater for herself-- not waiting for him-- so that was something. She had other clothes on under that; more than one layer.

He helped, holding each sleeve of her sweater, down on her arms, letting her pull her arms out of it as he helped.

She must be damned cold to do this so easily with the help of a complete stranger.

He peeled the sweater off over her head without asking permission, leaving her with her heavy shirt, also wet, as she leaned in against him to get more of his warmth. She was well enough dressed for windy and cold weather, with three good layers of clothing, but she'd not dressed for *this* weather.

The mist that had been over everything earlier that morning, presaging a better day than this, had been misleading. It had also dampened her, and she'd perspired; too overdressed at first, once the sun appeared. She'd peeled things off until the clouds had rolled in and the rain had come down, changing everything. She'd hurriedly put her various layers back on again, but not quickly enough. She'd been taken off guard.

She was wet all the way through. That sweater of hers wouldn't get any wetter now, so he pushed that down to cover his exposed lower legs which had been getting wet anyway from the rain and from walking through the longer grass that the sheep hadn't yet dealt with.

One down, several steps to go. He took a deep breath. On, to step two.

"I'll give you my sweater, it's warm and dry, but we'll have to get rid of this shirt too, or you won't get the full benefit of its protection."

He wondered where she'd draw the line.

She still wasn't objecting; still looking up into his face.

He wordlessly, and nervously, undid the buttons of her shirt, taking his time about it, ready for her to stop him at any time.

She didn't stop him as he worked down it, uncovering more of her body. There was nothing else beneath it, other than her bra!

He became more concerned for himself, than for her. When would she object?

He pulled the shirt up from inside her shorts… she had to raise herself from him for that, so that he could get at the remaining buttons. He paused before opening it from her to reveal her equally wet bra and her glistening wet skin.

She even helped him push each sleeve down her arms and off her. That shirt could sit on his bare legs too, for the moment, and get dry on them.

She was lightly sunburned after their hot summer. He couldn't see any tan lines from straps, or obvious areas of pale skin, but he wouldn't say anything about that. Maybe when she was alone up here, she got rid of everything up here and rambled the fells completely naked. There were times when he was up here in only his shorts, with the rest of his clothes in his pack.

He quashed that mind-blowing thought, but it had taken root.

She had a nice body. A very nice body. He would have liked to have been gamboling naked with her, all over this fell.

She knew he was admiring it. Damn. She'd been watching his face the whole time and must know what he was looking at, where, and what he was thinking; lusting after her.

He'd better not suggest that her bra should come off too, but it would have to, for her to get dry more quickly.

He tore his mind away from what he could see of her body.

She had to sit a little way back from him as he struggled to take off his own sweater, pulling it off over his head, disturbing everything around them as little as possible, re-oriented it between them, got her arms started into the sleeves, and then raised it to drop over her head to give her some protection and warmth.

He could see more of her as he did that, with her breasts more emphasized, standing out. He did things slowly, careful of what he touched. Everything about her was too interesting to him.

It was a relief that she hadn't stopped him or taken offense. She would get warmer now, feeling the benefit of its warmth almost immediately.

She would be about twenty, or twenty-one, he guessed, (his own age) and not exactly a girl... not with a body like that. She was behaving in an adult way, so far.

He asked permission for the next bold step, thinking that she would certainly refuse, and would prefer to stay wet. He explained why her bra should also come off, from under the sweater, but she didn't refuse, putting her hands on his shoulders so that he could do that for her, as they looked into each other's faces.

Holy....! She was giving him permission. she must be really cold.

His head was spinning. This couldn't be real... couldn't be happening to him. He was already feeling breathless. Seeing the way she looked at him with her so cold, so trusting, and so vulnerable, he just wanted to lean in and kiss her, but he also knew that he shouldn't, or he'd lose her trust; scare her. He was already scaring himself.

This next stage would have to be done very carefully, even with her permission.

He took another deep breath. Step three.

He reached around her, under the sweater to release her bra, watching her expression as he did that.

They were looking into each other's eyes as he did that; mutually plunging deeper into those depths as she read his innermost thoughts revealed to her there (difficult and confusing as they were), and as he tried to read hers. She was draining something out of him, but was giving him something in return, something much more valuable. A promise.

And it wasn't a promise of violence, either.

He didn't understand.

He snapped out of it. This was happening too quickly. She wasn't going to stop him no matter what he did, so he'd better be doubly careful.

Nonetheless, he'd flinched, as though she'd hit him for what he was thinking.

He'd given her some warning, so she knew what he was doing as he reached around her body, his face coming far too close to hers. His fingers were all thumbs as he fumbled to decipher the key to undoing it, out of his sight. There were two fasteners, maybe three. She'd need at least two, with these breasts. He unclipped it, letting it go slowly, then retreated, pulling both sides under her arms by the ends, being careful what he touched under there as she looked up into his face, studying him, ready to say something if he revealed too much of her, but she didn't, and he didn't either. He was doing only what was necessary. Nothing else.

She would object when she felt she needed to.

He held the sweater down as he reached up in front of it, and located the bottom of her bra, pulling at the middle of it, loosening it from her unseen, but nonetheless disturbing breasts, feeling things happening under there as they were released.

With some cautiously slow moves, he reached up with one hand… *careful now…* and pushed, and pulled her straps off her shoulders, fishing up one sleeve at a time for them with the other hand (exciting all by itself), pulling each one down into the sleeve and then over her wrist.

He'd never undressed any woman before, and he hoped he wasn't being too clumsy, or too obvious.

He moved slowly, explaining what he was doing and why, waiting for her objection, but she said nothing, so he continued with the other sleeve.

He must have been making sense to her.

Once the straps were off her arms, he went under the sweater again, and pulled at the middle of her bra, to be sure it was free from her breasts as the straps pulled back up and through the sleeves. He was careful not to touch her, or to reveal anything of her breasts, as he brought it out from under the sweater to lay on top of her shirt, keeping her covered the entire time. He felt relieved. He hadn't done too badly. They were substantial cups, and they'd been warm.

She'd said nothing the entire time, while his flushed face had been a complete open book for her to read.

Step three, completed. One step to go.

It had all been cleverly done, he thought.

He rubbed her back to dry it, and did more of the same on her shoulders and at the front, while carefully avoiding touching her directly, in the wrong places, and possibly unleashing a firestorm.

Working above and below her breasts as he did that to get her dry wasn't too difficult, causing her to look at him (there was nowhere else for her to look), ready to object if she needed to, except it had already gone too far for her to begin to object to anything.

He thought she could be smiling, when he looked at her, causing him to pause. He had to be mistaken about the smile.

She closed her eyes, waiting to see what he would suggest next. She didn't have that much more to be taken off.

The next stage would be the most awkward.

Again, he continued telling her what he was about to do, lifting at the bottom of his sweater, raising it a few inches to get at the top of her wet shorts. The shorts had received the brunt of the weather, with the rain driven almost horizontally as she'd walked. He unclipped them before he unzipped them, and slowly eased them down her legs and off her, leaving her wearing only her panties (which threatened to come with her shorts… indeed, had... come with them, until he'd stopped them), laying her shorts across his legs with her sweater, shirt, and bra, and then bringing her higher upon him to sit upon the legs of his own shorts. They would 'wick' the moisture out of her damp panties now that they were back where they should be... covering her.

He was dazed. He'd seen too much of her.

As her shorts had come down, and her panties, he'd seen… what hadn't he seen? There'd been hair of a distinctive character in a special place, and so much more becoming visible to him until he'd grabbed at her panties, already half-way down her thighs, and brought them back to where they should be. He couldn't unsee any of it. What was worse, she'd noticed, and yet had said nothing.

His mouth was dry, and he was beginning to feel light-headed. She should have rebelled long before now, but she hadn't.

Smarten up boy!

He'd better not apologize again for anything.

He'd deal with those wet clothes later. They wouldn't dry very quickly where they were on his legs, but they wouldn't get any wetter either.

Why she hadn't stopped him before now, he didn't understand. She wasn't in the least bit shy, and she was being very mature about all of it while he was behaving like a clumsy schoolboy.

He pulled her closer into him, feeling her arms between them until she moved them out of the way for herself, and pushed them around him to get even closer to him. She was feeling most of his warmth now, whereas he could feel how cold and damp she was, but at least he'd put her on the track to recovering.

He... was the one that might not recover.

His head was touching into her damp hair, until he retrieved her shirt to help get it dry, wiping over her neck too, then pulling her closer to him again as he went over her bare legs to dry them too.

Why wasn't she complaining?

There was something about her... something about her he couldn't explain. She'd tolerated too much, and without objection to what he'd been doing, and had done for her.

He'd have to think about that, if she'd let him.

A misplaced sense of humor.

He soon recovered his wits.

They needed to move beyond this. To do that, he needed to learn more about her; to get some kind of response out of her whichever way he could, to what he'd done.

"I don't think we need to remove any more of our clothes, do you? Unless you insist." He could hope, couldn't he?

His misplaced sense of humor would get him into trouble. Where was his reckless mouth taking him?

He was being mischievous, trying to get some response out of her… anything… then he continued.

"However, I think that, could become dangerous for us both." Truer words were never spoken.

He should shut up, or he'd scare her. It was already dangerous, but she didn't seem either scared or ready to battle him away. She seemed amused even. Perhaps she perceived him as being more adult and trustworthy than he actually felt.

She made a noise that sounded like a chuckle against his chest, and he felt her shake her head.

Unbelievable! She hadn't got scared over that comment or what had happened already? She must have brothers, or she was familiar with that kind of risqué humor. Or... and this bothered him... she knew all about him. Brothers! He tried again.

"Good. I'm in enough trouble as it is."

And he was gradually digging himself in, deeper.

It would be even more tricky and troublesome, reversing all of this, especially when she struggled in front of him to put her bra back on. It would be interesting to see how she would do that with him helping (he would always want to help), and with them as close together as they were.

He would want to watch that. Even to help, but that was still some time away. He stopped his mind from continuing down that track.

Talking was safer... if he was careful what he said... and it might help him relax. But she wasn't saying much of anything in response.

She, this woman, was different from those he usually encountered. He sensed that, and it bothered him in ways he couldn't easily define. She'd already seen into his soul and it hadn't frightened her.

He could soon be in a lot more trouble, the way he was feeling... out of his depth... not knowing why she was trusting him, instead of complaining or resisting him.

He'd never had to do anything like this for any woman before. She must be very mature not to be too concerned about what he'd done, so far.

She may have understood that last comment too, but he hoped not. He *was*, in trouble, but that was his own, uniquely male, problem.

He bent his legs to bring his feet under their cover more, and to take her weight off him in an awkward and tender place before she objected to changes in his body as he leaned back with her against the hard boulder behind them. It took the pressure off him there. She might have detected that about him with her having so little clothing on, and with her sitting almost directly upon that part of his, clothing or not. His imagination didn't help, nor his knowledge that she was covered only by a single, delicate piece of clothing.

She might have been able to feel him prodding up at her like a volcano about to erupt. He was that way because of her. She'd notice for sure if that happened to him, and he ejaculated in his excitement.

That aspect of any man was usually enough to concern any woman detecting that about his body if she wasn't on the same wavelength as him. They didn't know enough about each other to be anywhere near that advanced stage of relaxed intimacy.

She would have to say something about her own physical condition soon, to let him know what more he could do to help her get warm, except he'd done all he could, until she was warmer, and her clothes drier, which would be the next major step.

It was still raining hard. They could hear it drumming against their single covering and running down it, but where they were, seemed fairly-well sheltered and was out of the wind and cold. It was even getting warm, but that might be for other reasons.

He began to recover his wits.

It seemed to be one of those downpours that was likely to go on for hours; the tail-end of some storm or other blown across the Atlantic. It was getting cold enough for snow too. Out on the fells like this, was not the place to be caught out and exposed when this happened.

They had no choice about how things would have to go at this moment. She needed to get warm and he needed to do something about getting her clothes, dry, if he could. As well as to get his mind off this other problem he had.

He was recovering.

"Come in closer if you can, and get the benefit of my warmth. There is no point in us being shy at this stage. I think you know that I'm not that much of a threat for you. It isn't as though we can't control ourselves."

Really? Had he actually said that?

He wasn't sure what had made him add those two stupid comments at the end. He was unable to control himself in a way that he couldn't discuss with her, and as a horny male, very much out of control, he would always be a threat to her.

She seemed to agree with that request however, and got closer to him, not offended, or scared, by his telling comments. She seemed to be one of the least shy women he had ever come across, but she was still wet and cold, and that would dull her sense of caution.

He was even more curious about her now.

He cautiously pulled at her hips to get her closer into him. She had broad and warm hips, and he felt her panties move under his hand as he pulled at her there. He could even see how they moved.

There was nothing he could do about that, but it bothered him to be touching her like that. She didn't fight him away despite him being so close to… everything that a woman usually fought to protect. He raised both of his hands to her head to give her some warmth from them too, as he firmly swept water off her hair, explaining what he was doing and why.

He tried to take his mind off what he was thinking and feeling. He was too nervous.

His hands would be out of the way and safer up here. Safer for them both. He could feel her breasts scrunched up against his chest. That, didn't help.

They could talk now. He needed her to say something to lift him off this hook he was twisting on.

"What were you doing out on the fell in this?"

Her voice was muffled in his shirt.

"It wasn't like this when I set out this morning. It was promising to be sunny." It had been an unarguable response. He'd thought the same thing.

"I walk this fell most of the summer when the weather is good, but this was the first time I've been caught out so badly." She said nothing about wandering it in a half-naked state, as he still wanted to imagine her doing. He couldn't ask her about that.

She had a nice voice, if deadened by his shirt. It had looked like a good day when he'd set out too, so he could say nothing.

She fidgeted on him, possibly still detecting his awkward condition. He shouldn't have been like that, but he was, because of the way his mind was working and with her so close to him in his arms and half naked.

She smelled good, too.

He shouldn't have thought of that. This could only end in disaster for him.

She fidgeted. "I must still be heavy on you." At least she managed to avoid speaking of the obvious; poking at her, and castigating him for his lack of bodily control. Somehow, she managed to seem concerned for him, rather than alarmed for herself.

He wanted to tell her not to be afraid. He couldn't always help the way his body behaved, especially not when he had a beautiful, half-clothed woman in his arms, sitting on his lap, and one with the body of a goddess. Only an idiot would draw her attention to that. This, was also a first for him.

Although maybe she should be afraid.

He began to be concerned on her behalf, wondering what she was thinking about this, and about him and what he had done for her. It seemed important for him to know that.

"You're not that heavy on me just yet. You need to get warmer. If you get to be too heavy (or become concerned about what you feel of me), I'll let you sit between my legs on my pack and lean back into me."

The decision would be in her hands.

But then he'd still have a problem about where to put his hands.

"At least it's dry, and I took my lunch out of it before we sat on it." He moved her shoulder bag under his legs too, just in case she became concerned enough to take him up on that offer.

She asked about him, instead, keeping the needed dialogue going between them.

"What about you? Why are you on this fell? No one ever comes up here. Weeks can go by without me seeing anyone."

He put the back of his hand under the edge of his sweater on her midriff to sense her temperature, feeling the top of her panties against his hand. They were low on her, and he could sense that hair too. She didn't even flinch; looking into his eyes the whole time. He removed his hand slowly.

She said nothing about that trespass, but she had flinched and glanced up at him, wondering.

"Sorry. I didn't mean to be clumsy."

He had to stay disconnected.

He told himself that, over and over again. She was cool to his touch. He should touch her thighs too, to check them, if he dared.

However, she would tell him if she was still feeling *really* cold anywhere, and she could tell him off if he went too far.

He reached out and touched her thigh anyway, resting his hand on it for just a few seconds, feeling that she was still cold.

She seemed to understand why he'd done that.

He tried to ignore what he was feeling and answered her earlier question.

"I came up here for a few days to collect mineral samples from some of the old lead-mine spoil heaps; whatever I can find, but I was just getting to where the old mines were when this storm began, and then I saw you, and you looked like you needed help."

He hadn't noticed how the thunder and lightning had already gone by them as he'd struggled to deal with her. He'd had to change his plans at that moment, knowing that it might get difficult.

Understatement of the year!

She concurred. "I did need your help. I haven't seen it come down like that for a long time. Thank you, and you are warm. I'll soon get more comfortable. It would have been a miserable walk home with me as wet as I was."

She might not have made it at all if she'd got any colder and wetter. It would still be a miserable walk home if he didn't help her.

He would help her.

"You're getting warmer now." He'd touched her again. Her middle was warming. She no longer flinched when he touched her. He'd touched her there twice now, as well as holding her on her back, under his sweater, and she'd said nothing. She was warm everywhere she was in contact against him. It was her extremities that were a problem. They should be warmer.

Nonetheless, there was some improvement. She'd stopped shivering and was snuggling into him more confidently now, and with her arms around him, even pushing confidently into his shirt.

He pulled her closer, leaving his large hand resting on her cool thigh.

She seemed to have learned enough about him to relax, but he would never learn enough about her.

It was a matter of priorities. The need for warmth dulled a lot of fears and woke one up to what was needed. One had to experience things like this: difficulties, tragedies, to see the value in life, especially when you came closest to finding how fragile life really was, as she had done. It woke you up, like watching a good hanging!

At least she wasn't so scared now—if she'd ever been scared of him—which was a 'positive' about all of this.

Why wasn't she scared of him?

With them lying together like this, in a way two strangers never usually did, it would be a challenge. He would have to start more of this verbal exchange and keep it going.

'My name is Caldwell. James Caldwell. Jim."

"Jim, James." She paused as she digested his name. "Hi. Pleased to meet you. I'm Louise Prescott. Botanist, general naturalist in the old tradition." She explained. "I wander and collect things."

Her mother would have a shock when she brought this man home with her off the fell, instead of those harmless things her daughter usually collected on her walks. She would not see this man as harmless, because he wasn't, not considering the effect he was already having on her daughter.

They wouldn't shake hands. There was no need for that formality with what they were already doing, touching each other almost everywhere.

"You must be staying at the Inn in Blaethorpe." She already knew that.

She felt him nod.

"I think I saw you yesterday up here. I live on the other side of the fell from there, with my family. If you draw a straight line between the Inn and my home, on the map, then we are sitting on the midpoint of that line and about as high on this fell as you can get."

She was opening up to him, which she wouldn't have done if she'd been scared or angry with him.

He felt relieved. He also now knew where she lived. They both were left with a lot to think about.

Tell me a little about yourself, James.

"How do you feel, Louise? More comfortable? Warmer?" That was the first time he'd used her name.

It brought them closer together.

"Both of those, thank you. I wasn't looking forward to trying to get home in the condition I was in, but it won't be so bad once I get warmer and drier."

"I'll see to you getting home." There would be no question of that.

"Thank you." She was thanking him too much, although for her, it would never be enough. She hadn't realized how badly off she'd been until he'd helped her, despite his bold attack. It had been necessary.

"As we are caught up together in this… inescapably… difficult situation…" she was able to laugh about it … "would you mind telling me something about yourself… James? I prefer, James, to Jim."

He liked the sound of that.

"There's not much to tell. I'm twenty-one, and still at university. I have two sisters, one older, one younger. They generally kept me in line while I was growing up."

As sisters did.

Her hands were inside his shirt, next to his skin, and pushing around him, slowly rising up his back. She was making him nervous, and more excited.

"I tend to be shy around most women. They can see right through me. Very unnerving. I never had time for a girlfriend." Why on earth was he telling her that?

He was playing himself down. But good news …about the girlfriend.

As he talked, with her head close to his—close enough that they were breathing upon each other as he held her close—his hands were behind her, under her sweater and touching her as she was touching him; moving, as hers were doing, up on her back to the same level as her breasts.

If only… but getting closer all the time.

She smelled… like a blast of aphrodisiacal hormones, turning him on a roasting spit…. What wouldn't he give to be even closer to her? Sharing the same skin. It wouldn't take much a change. One or two very small adjustments would do it. She might not notice him going into her.

Like hell she wouldn't. He should stop thinking like that!

She must know how she was affecting him. That personal problem of his was still there, but as long as he talked, she might not notice what was happening to him.

He eventually ran out of things to tell her, having told her enough for now.

"What about you, Louise. What should I know about you?" (that he didn't already know.) He already knew that she had a fabulous body and was confident in herself.

He could ask now.

She chuckled. "You already know too much about me. You undressed me and left me almost entirely defenceless." Her panties didn't count. She *was*, defenceless in that way. "I was concerned for a moment that you intended to take everything off me."

It had been too close to actually happening.

She didn't seem that concerned about it, and for all the cover her panties provided it wouldn't have mattered much if he had.

"I might not have objected and then where would we be."

She might not have objected? Oh, hell!

Her describing that so calmly, and even laughing about it set his head churning again. It didn't help his other problem either.

He hadn't intended taking her panties off. His temperature had soared as he'd seen them coming down with her shorts. He'd grabbed at them at the last moment, stopping their descent, and had lifted them back before she noticed. Except she'd noticed. She noticed everything but didn't always say what she was thinking.

She told him as much about her… her brothers, her parents, as he had told her. She was also freshly graduated, as he was, and was the same age as him. They were even at the same university and had been for the last three years. That surprised him.

"I wonder why we didn't meet at university with us both going to the same one, and with us graduating in the same year."

"It's not that surprising, James. There are almost ten thousand students, and with us being in different departments with no overlapping courses, we would never have come that close to each other to meet." True.

"However, I think we're making up for that now."

She was right. They surely were, but they still had a lot of ground to catch up.

She wasn't sure, but had he just kissed her on the neck, under her ear? It had felt like it.

No. That was just her imagination, and wishful thinking (pity), but she could put her face into his neck and breathe in more of his male smell that was on all of his clothes, and was driving her nuts. She could kiss him there too; a brief, glancing kind of kiss that he might not notice. It seemed to be called for. It would be different if she did it.

When they slept together, they would be like this. As close as this. Even closer, and there would be much more happening between them. Where had that thought come from?

She didn't know.

He must have thoughts like that too, else he wouldn't be as aroused for her as he clearly was. He was also embarrassed to be like that. Better and better.

She'd never considered anything like this happening with any man before, so this was a first in every way for her, as it seemed to be for him. He had that effect on her, just as she was affecting him in a notable way, but she couldn't talk about that… what she knew, and could feel of him.

"So, where do we go from here, James?" She would at least see what he would suggest.

He liked the way she used his name.

"We'll need to reverse all of what we did; eventually, when your clothes are a lot dryer, though we'll need to make some changes to get them drying. I'll let you wear most of my drier clothes, and I can wear your shirt and that denim jacket. They looked too big on you, and might fit me, but your shorts won't."

She could have his underwear too, to help keep her warm and dry, if she wouldn't be repelled by that thought.

"You can wear this slicker, once I get it down to size again, and I can even put a belt around it to stop it blowing off you." The wind was still strong. "I'll get you home."

She'd look good, walking into the house dressed entirely in his clothes and him in hers. And with him the way he was… aroused, and obviously so. Her mother really would have a fit.

He'd been that way all of the time he'd helped her, and he was still that way, and she knew it. Her mother would see everything, and would guess at a lot more.

"The shirt and seater are my brother's. They'll fit you. But you'll get wet."

"Better me than you, and we'll be moving fast."

She needed to get a lot of other things out of the way between them first, in the remaining time they would need to stay here for her to fully recover.

If she had courage enough to do it.

He was a once-in-a-lifetime opportunity to come her way. She knew already how she felt. He was a 'keeper', and she wasn't going to waste this moment and lose him… not for a second.

She could get started on that, even now. He, wouldn't, being so shy and afraid of scaring her, so she would have to.

Learning even more about him.

She moved again. "I must be uncomfortable for you. I'm no lightweight."

She may have detected his worsening problem again (damned hormones), but she didn't say anything directly about it. That would have been embarrassing, possibly... no, undoubtedly..., and even more embarrassing for him, than for her.

She was proving to be a woman of strong character and unfazed by almost anything; confident in herself.

"If I'm hurting you sitting on you like this (she knew about his problem), I can move to sit between your legs as you suggested, but I'm not sure how that would work. Or,"—she thought about it— "I could turn to face you and put my legs over yours and lean into you. That way, we will be closer together, for warmth's sake. Except...." There was a longish pause. She didn't continue.

She shouldn't be suggesting such tempting things.

Except..., that wouldn't have removed her from the problem at all, but would have put her even closer to it, and to... 'trouble-of-the-first-kind'. The wrong kind, with her legs apart and on either side of him like that... and with her panties not protecting her at all now, or hiding much. They would be too close to getting into real trouble.

It didn't seem to concern her too much, to suggest it herself.

That could become even more awkward for them both than it was now, especially if he became aroused any more than he was, and without her heavy shorts protecting her from sensing more of him. He began to perspire.

Her panties alone, would be no protection at all, and if they moved out of the way, as she herself moved...? They were already partially out of the way.

Just thinking about it was exciting for them both, but he didn't know that about her. It was his... unique problem.

She may even have heard him groan at the thought, suffering as he was. She certainly saw him close his eyes.

If they had known each other much better, and over some weeks, they might have been able to laugh about this... closeness; simulating sex together; ideally positioned for it. However, one didn't joke about things like this without knowing each other very well, and even risking it going a lot further in a mutually agreed upon way.

If he made any jocular suggestion like that, he might send her screaming off the fell without her clothes, and he had told her his name, and where he was staying.

The police would be looking for him after that. Everything would be incriminating no matter what he said... him, having her critical clothing, and her pack... would be all they would see.

She wouldn't do that anyway. It was too cold to panic like that, and she was made of sterner stuff than that.

He'd better not tell her about those thoughts.

He could even see them coupling in that way, doing that, with her legs around him, both parts juxtaposed at first, then fusing slowly together as she sank down onto him. There would be problems no matter what they did to get dry and warm in this confined space, so he had to learn to get control of himself and to watch his tongue and his imagination.

He smiled at her. "No matter how we do it, it is likely to get personal and embarrassing in some way, for one or even for both of us as we move around."

There he went again. Too damned honest. But he was only telling the truth.

She even agreed with him, blundering onto dangerous ground for herself with a telling chuckle. "I know. It's already been personal. You got my bra off so cleverly (you naughty boy, you), and also managed to control yourself. One piece of clothing to go, which I already came close to losing once, and then my goose really will be cooked. However, I think you might be a gentleman. Lucky me."

She kissed him under his chin. "Thank you. You didn't try and take advantage of me too much. At least, I don't think so." She looked up into his face, her eyes glistening. She even smiled, robbing her next words of any fear.

"I thought you were going to, at one stage, and then I realized how shy and embarrassed you were."

He had been that, right enough.

"You didn't do too badly, apart from blushing. Your blushing told me all about you. I knew then that I wasn't in any real danger from you."

He remembered... when he'd been struggling with her bra and her shorts. She'd seen his alarmed attentiveness to her, especially when he'd seen her panties heading down her legs and had intervened to stop them.

So, she knew about him, and had known enough not to be concerned about him. Damn!

But at the same time... thank goodness for that.

He didn't know whether to be thankful, or disappointed, but he had a comeback for that.

"And how would I have done that... let myself lose control... (in some undefined way) and have survived? I really would like to know... for the next time we do this." He was being very brave.

She could hardly believe what she was hearing.

His irrepressible sense of humor would get him into trouble if he was not careful, but he was merely coming back at her.

She laughed. "I don't know. I'll have to think about it and let you know... for the next time. You managed well enough and didn't let anything stop you or hold you back. I'd say you managed quite well, even cleverly, as you got my bra off without me complaining. That move, asking like that... suggesting... was efficiently done. Most men don't know how to do that without being told, or shown. And I didn't even fight you away as you did that, but I was covered all of the time. Thank you for that."

He'd watched one of his elder sister's friends, struggling to take off her uncomfortable bra, outside, in their garden, while she'd still been wearing a shirt. She'd not been bothered in the slightest that he was watching. He'd been spellbound watching that, waiting in anticipation for a glimpse of her minuscule breasts. Such disappointment! Her breasts had been really small, however. Nothing like these! Even egg cups would have been too big for those. *Nothing like these.*

Louise also seemed to have a sense of humor that matched his own. It was a good sign that she was relaxing.

"You could have stopped me easily at any time, Louise. You just needed to say something. Although… did I scare you? I know that I can be quite intense when things need to be done, and I have a tendency to bull my way forward. My sisters tell me that, all of the time."

So that was how he had known what to do with her bra. Sisters again.

"I tried not to be… too pushy or attentive to you, but I was having difficulty knowing what to do… how far I needed to go to get you warm. You even seemed to find my embarrassment, funny. You are… different."

He added to his attempt at honesty.

"You are beautiful too. Confident in yourself."

He blushed. "Sorry, I shouldn't have said that about you being beautiful, but you are."

He kicked himself, metaphorically. He was sounding disingenuous; too flattering. A man would say almost anything to any nearly naked woman who was letting him undress her, just to get closer to her and to get more clothes off her.

She didn't take offense or tell him off.

"Thank you, James. You sound as though you mean it. You didn't scare me; not after the first couple of minutes, and you seemed to know what you were doing. You were persuasive about it, and I was cold, so I didn't say anything to stop you, though I was ready to, if I sensed the wrong thing."

She continued. "I have a younger and an older brother, so I know what happens with them when they… er... get… that way… hormonal. They get too obvious… (just like him), and I am only their inconsequential sister. They're not shy around girls either, or backward. The girls tell me. I doubt that you are much different from them. They seem to be insensitive, horny sods (*just like him*), so I sometimes need to tell them off and let them know how they should behave around a girl, but they are lost causes."

Especially Trevor, her elder brother.

Damn. She knew about her brothers' antics, so she knew all about him!

She would still be able to detect his body, the way it was. *Damn, again.* That would scare any woman. Except she didn't seem so scared. Hell, she was mature enough to know what it was all about. She probably knew more than he did. He'd better get control and keep himself out of her way, but he couldn't get to that rebel to adjust where it was with her lying on him, and he would be too obvious if he tried to do it. He couldn't tell her what he needed to do--to resettle the beast--and he couldn't ask her to do that adjustment for him… no matter how he ached for her to do that.

"I'm probably not much different from your brothers." Not different at all.

She let out a convulsive shiver.

Her exposed legs would still be cold. He touched them, high on her thighs and checked. They were still cold.

"I'll tell you what… two birds with one stone." He was feeling bold and brave enough to go along with some of what she'd suggested earlier. "I'll open up my shirt so you can get even closer to me, if you won't panic."

Another layer of clothing between them, gone.

He was likely the one who would panic.

They would be chest, to chest, even with that sweater between them, and they would be even closer to being intimate down there too, if she turned more to face him.

It was almost what she'd suggested, earlier.

"If you turn to face me and put your legs over mine, as you just suggested, and move in, close to me, lie upon me… your legs can come close into my side, inside my shirt. You can get your thighs warm against my sides as you trap my shirt, and you can even lie into me as much as you can. That should help."

They were almost on the same song sheet.

And forget about the overwhelming temptations with her in his arms, lying on him like that; open below, inviting, vulnerable.

It was her turn to be outspoken this time, asking one of those questions that women asked, while they didn't need to ask it.

She even blushed, bashfully. "Will that be safe for me, do you think, after our earlier conversation about my almost non-existent panties?" She was not entirely sure where they were at that moment.

She knew it wouldn't be safe at all, but she obviously didn't care. She had a dangerous sense of humor with that… not-so-innocent, comment that told him she knew all about him, and that he was only a wuss, when it came to real women. And what did she mean, telling him that about her almost non-existent panties? She was in control, mostly.

"I doubt that I was comfortable for you, sitting on you *there*," she figuratively fluttered her hand, rather than speak directly of the devil or give it a name… if he gave that part of himself a name… "and if we do that, it would…."

Yes, it certainly would!

"My mother warned me about that… having my legs apart with a man between them, *and* being more than half undressed."

Her mother wouldn't know the half of it, and that her teaching had fallen on barren ground.

She didn't seem to be too concerned about that.

He almost choked over her dangerous sense of humor. He wanted to laugh, but he knew that he shouldn't. It was far too serious for that, and was becoming more serious by the minute.

She was absolutely, unexpectedly, unbelievably… everything wonderful he could think of.

His body still was that way, and… she… knew it. She was causing it, with comments and observations like that.

He laughed in disbelief. "You don't lack courage, I'll give you that, to discuss such personal things."

Or, she had a reckless sense of humor.

"However, we'd both have to be naked for that (what a dizzying thought to share with her and to see how she would respond), and I think... that would be a step too far." He didn't think anything of the kind. There was only one piece of her clothing separating her from that.

At least, a step too far for one of us. But he could hope.

She came back at him. "I almost am naked, thanks to you. Not so far to go; just these flimsy little things between us, wherever they are." She even sighed, as though in regret. "And you think me beautiful too. Flatterer. Seduction 101. How to remove all of a woman's clothing without her objecting or even detecting that they were gone. Step one, get her miserably wet and cold. Step two, speak softly and be persuasive. I think you would graduate with honors, James. Not far to go to graduate *summa cum laude*."

He couldn't believe what she was saying.

She shouldn't have reminded him of that... about how close she was to being naked...and intimate... not with her lying on him, so close like this, and her panties just a whisper of a breath away from being off her.

"I think we both knew what I was doing and how necessary it was. At least, I assessed it as being necessary. You could have objected if it wasn't, but you didn't."

She agreed. "It *was,* necessary. I was too cold and uncomfortable to complain, so thank you. You shouldn't apologize for what couldn't have been helped."

He wasn't sure what she was referring to... getting her out of her wet clothes, or the fact that he was getting more aroused by the minute, thinking of those 'flimsy panties' as she'd called them, and them, ready to evaporate magically from between them if they both willed it to happen. Maybe they'd already gone.

He wasn't going to apologize for what he couldn't help, especially when she seemed to be deliberately drawing his attention to his lack of control, as well as her own state of undress, and making him even worse by the minute, with this line of conversation.

He shouldn't blame her for this problem.

He tried to refocus.

"Putting all of those things aside; the major consideration at this moment, is to get you warm, and to get your clothes dryer than they are.

"I can try and wring them out, if we can develop some space in here, but not just yet (they were getting warmer over his legs), and then we can maybe eat some of my lunch, while we negotiate a way forward and decide how to get you home without you getting miserably wet again."

And without doing any serious damage to each other.

She'd gone quiet now, mulling over what he'd suggested... negotiating... also known as playing into her hands.

He'd opened the door for her. 'The time had come', the walrus said. Time to be decisive. He couldn't know what siren he'd unleashed. Except he'd soon find out.

It (that obvious part of him) was an embarrassing and awkward difficulty between them, for them to deal with... especially for him, but only because it was in the wrong place.

She knew what the right place was, and so did he, but he wasn't going to do anything about it.

It was only a few centimeters away from where it needed to be, yet they were seemingly a world apart.

How could she possibly think like this? Never in a thousand years would she ever have believed that anything like this could be possible for her, or would be even briefly entertained, but she had to believe it now.

She knew she had fallen in love in an instant of time, and that he had done the same thing, but he would not easily admit it so soon, or do anything about it.

He would strive to be a gentleman, of course, and try to protect her from learning any more about him in that way; but that would never do.

Oh, how, her life had changed; and within minutes of them meeting, and of him beginning to undress her so boldly, overcoming his shy reluctance to do so.

That, was a delight for her to see; his confusion; his embarrassment; his obvious condition... just because of her.

That, put her in control.

She had to consider the possibilities, as revolutionary as they were, before they were lost to them forever.

It would be so easy to do... if she dared. However, nothing ventured, nothing gained.

If she were to put it (that obvious part of his again... it was still there, knocking at her door) in the right place on her body... if she dared to do that so soon after them meeting... it would not only be out of the way from between them; discomforting them both (physically and mentally) as it was, with it nudging and prodding at her much of the time, but it would also put them on a very different, intimate track, altogether. It was close to happening, and had been even closer to them joining in unholy matrimony, from time to time. He wanted to... or he wouldn't be like that. She wanted to.

He was, undoubtedly, too shy to do it, so she would have to find that courage for him.

They had to fuck! (what a shocking thing to think about!). *They absolutely had to fuck each other, and as soon as possible. After that, they could talk about making 'love'* (which is what it would be, every time after that)*, but she would have to the one to get that difficult, 'squishy' bit... the first move... that, 'fucking', bit, out of the way from between them.*

Progression.

She had an idea... leading on to that greater goal. More clothing had to come off.

"This will work better between us if you put both layers of your sweater over my back as I lean into you, inside your shirt. That will get us even closer together and give me more of your warmth."

It sure would—bare skin; her breasts, directly touching against his bare skin and, fortunately, she was the one suggesting it, not him. He felt as though he was being carried away by something he couldn't fight against.

Things were likely to get out of control if that happened, but... she'd been the one who suggested it.

He gave in and helped her take his sweater off over her head once she'd got started on it, revealing her breasts fully to him this time, almost poking him in the eye with her proud nipples as she carefully assessed his response to that bold move in his expression. She giggled mischievously. She didn't want to shock him too much and possibly lose him but she knew what she was doing, and why.

He almost died, wanting to reach out and touch; to mouth at them, kiss them.

He knew that the cold did that to them. Made them erect. He had to close his eyes for a moment. She didn't seem to care what effect she was having on him.

God! They were magnificent.

This had to be a dream, but he knew that it wasn't.

She was watching his face the whole time as he'd pulled his shirt apart to get this moving as she'd suggested, liking what she saw of him there too. There was not an ounce of fat on him. He helped her fold his sweater and to bring it around her to cover her back as she changed the position of her legs.

He was hypnotized; unable to take his eyes off her breasts, watching her sit back on him (very dangerous maneuver, that), placing her feet close beside his knees, and well aware of what pushed up at her, beneath her. She laid forward on him, her cold thighs touching against his side, as he'd suggested, (or had she suggested that? Did it matter who? Neither of them was thinking clearly about this), and as he brought his shirt sides up to be trapped around her thighs.

He was fixated on her breasts the entire time. They were nothing like those of his sisters, as interesting as those were to him when he glimpsed them by accident. Those, were small in comparison to these substantial orbs.

Her panties weren't doing much of anything to hide her now with her legs as wide apart as they were. They were not covering her... barely covering her at all... pulling away from her as she inched closer and leaned into him, revealing some hair, and even a hint of her labia. He felt weak. Her mother had been right to warn her about this.

The top of her panties was opening up at the front too, to let him see down into them as the gusset of them hung up on his rough legs and were being moved around in a decidedly enervating way for him, as she inched forward to get closer to him. Another few inches, and they would be off her, or as good as off.

His mind just about exploded as she laid back down upon his chest.

Her bare breasts: solid... firm, were now pushing directly onto his equally naked chest, and her panties… she might as well not have been wearing any! They were another casualty, moving them ever closer to actual intimacy now, and she didn't seem to care!

If the zip of his shorts relaxed at all… or failed…! He was below her now, with that still worsening problem of his, so she couldn't detect that about him as easily as she had before, but even so, it was loudly proclaiming its presence.

He was vibrantly conscious of all of that, driving him slowly over the edge as he became even more aroused. He wanted to touch all of her.

Why was she doing this to him?

He recovered his wits enough to bring her damp shirt up and over her back onto the sweater over her back. It would dry out there, better than it would on his legs.

He could say nothing, struck dumb for the moment. She didn't have an ounce of shyness in her.

He left her own wet sweater and jacket over his lower legs to protect those, and to get them partially dry. He'd see to them later.

He slid further down with her, to lie more prone under her as much as the rock, and their awkward 'seating', would allow. It was bloody uncomfortable, but he'd survive!

She could lie on him more easily now, and she was also a smidgen farther removed from the 'trouble' zone, but it didn't help the way he was feeling. He'd seen and felt too much of her for his own good.

What he'd sensed of her changing mood about him didn't help, either.

He had enough wit left to pull his sweater farther up her back to cover her still-damp hair and neck, and then pulled her shirt down, to cover the back of her panties—wherever they were... they were not where he touched—then brought *her* own damp sweater up to cover her exposed buttocks too. No gaps allowed. Her panties were not where they should have been! He'd felt that. They didn't seem to be there, but he hadn't seen her take them off as she'd moved.

He was already too warm by far and was becoming more confused and breathless at what she was doing to him.

He checked her again on her buttocks where she'd been coldest before.

Her upper legs were less cold, so he was having some effect on her. She was having a much bigger effect on him, however, but he couldn't talk to her about that.

She knew, of course.

She chuckled, nervously, over some thought she had, and she sounded… amused, rather than offended by what was happening.

He felt higher at the edge of his sweater, feeling the side of her breasts against his hands. He paused.

She'd raised herself from him, just an inch… inviting? If he wanted to slide his hands in between them and hold them...?

Was she inviting him to touch her there? It seemed she was.

He couldn't believe it.

He'd heard a whisper of a sound in his ear, like a breeze that sounded like…. *'They feel warm, but you should check, please'.*

She wanted him to do that? She was inviting him to check them for her? Maybe he was losing his hearing, or imagining it.

At least she wasn't fighting him off her.

His hands were warm, so he slid them between their bodies, below her breasts--they would be safer there-- as she held herself away from him.

There was that whisper again. *'Chicken!'* *You know what I want."*

He couldn't believe it, but he hadn't misheard.

She was the one who took hold of his hands and moved them up to sit full on her breasts as she raised herself from him. He did what she wanted... shyly... tentatively; resisting her at first, waiting for her to object, despite her being the one suggesting it, but she didn't object, so he gave in and held them more confidently.

If she wasn't careful this really would get out of hand, though it was already galloping along that way. She still said nothing, except for that sigh, again. She probably needed him to touch, to verify that she was still cool, there. He willingly obliged. His hands were now full upon her breasts, feeling her hard nipples under his palms. He waited for her to change her mind, or for some objection.

It didn't come.

She kissed him under his ear, instead and snuggled closer to him!

"Your hands are so warm. Thank you."

She shouldn't have done that!

Her breasts were warm too.

"My upper legs and my buttocks are still cool."

She wanted him to touch her there to find out about them, too?

He moved, though he didn't want to. He could always come back to her breasts, later.

He moved his hands, sliding them down under their clothing and even into the back of her panties to touch her cheeks. Her cheeks were cool, but at least she still had panties.

What the hell! This was her idea, so he was just doing what she wanted.

He was getting breathless.

"Why are you doing this, Louise?"

She kissed him, smiling at him.

"You know, why. Because it is called for, and because it is necessary, James. For both of us. We both know that."

Necessary in what way? "But...but... you don't know me."

She laid a finger on his lips.

"I do know you. I know all about you that I need to know. I knew you within the first five minutes of you approaching me, just as you knew about me. I saw it in your eyes."

He couldn't believe what he was hearing.

He responded. "I thought that feeling was unique to me... one-sided. That was why I was flustered, and so shy and why I tried to be careful about what I did and said."

"I know. And that was considerate of you. But we don't need to be that way with each other anymore." She moved herself, repositioning her legs beside him opening herself up below to his forthcoming discovery of her. He would soon catch on.

When he realized what she wanted him to do....

"Come, touch me, everywhere, James, and I mean everywhere. Learn about me. We have to make love before we leave here."

Had she just said that? Holy...! Who was this woman?

She fidgeted again, bringing her legs up even higher on him. She continued to kiss him and to sigh audibly, liking what he was doing. He wasn't sure he'd heard her over the pounding in his head.

Had she just said, 'keep going, please,' or was that his troubled imagination leading him on into more trouble. This wouldn't end well for either of them if he wasn't careful.

She guided his hands again, pushing them to where she wanted them to be.

He gave in to what she wanted, and pushed further, feeling her panties sliding down on the back of his hands.

"That's it." She snuggled closer to him and sighed.

He gave up trying to second guess her. She wanted him to do this, and to do even more; seeming not to care about protecting her virtue from him, but even wanting him to do something drastic with it. He desperately needed to oblige her, now that she'd given him a green light.

He checked lightly between her legs from behind her, not wanting to be too pushy, at first. She could still object and stop him anytime she changed her mind, but she didn't. Everything was warm, welcoming, and inviting to him. Moist, too.

Oh, what the hell!

He kissed her.

"Are you sure about this, Louise?" He could at least ask again, to be sure.

"Yes. I am sure, and so are you. I hope you don't think that this is always how I am, because it's not, and I've never let any man undress me before, or touch my breasts, or even do this to me. You are the only one; the first. I've never got this close to someone who excited me before as you do."

It was the same for him.

She shouldn't have told him that. She was in his head the same way he seemed to be in hers, giving him a license to mercilessly plunder her. It was mutual.

She moved her legs apart for him, to encourage him further.

His temperature was rocketing up now, and he was already harder than he could ever remember.

He was slow and gentle with what he was doing, learning about her, feeling hair on his finger ends, and then, as she seemed to relax upon him more, even rotating her hips to open herself up to his invited inspection—completely mind-blowing in itself—a moist space, that he definitely needed to know more about.

He investigated slowly, moving along her vulva, letting her feel what he was doing, taking his time about it.

Yes, he was touching her along there, and she wasn't stopping him.

He'd have to wake up soon from this dream.

This was no dream. She wanted him to learn about her, so he gave in to what she wanted. He could resist only so far.

He learned what he could, feeling her become even more moist with his touch, and her breathing and agitation becoming more noticeable. This would soon be more than he could bear. He felt her respond when his fingers came up to her vagina, touching at her there, needing to find out everything now.

She wanted more of him than just touching. She wanted him to learn so much more about her there, too, as well as to touch her breasts.

He needed another pair of hands!

This was running away with him and gathering a momentum of its own.

She was tight, and tense with what he was doing. She'd flinched when he'd gone into her even just a little with his finger. Unless… unless she was still a virgin. But she wasn't behaving like a virgin-- unfamiliar with any of this-- and she wasn't stopping him or fighting him off her as she should have been.

She wanted, needed him to learn all about her.

This need that she had for him, confused him. Women didn't usually go so aggressively after any man; not the women he was aware of.

Her warm breath on his neck, seemed to tell him more. She was also making other, approving sounds, and was moving herself down there as though to encourage him.

Emboldened, he continued, persisting, as she seemed to want, inserting his longest middle finger a little more… as she relaxed more, both of them encountering some difficulty. She was snug on him. She may not have a hymen; few women this age did, but she was still very tight on his finger, as a virgin would be.

He wouldn't dare ask.

She was still tense… then she relaxed more, under this unfamiliar assault. He continued. He had to pause again, letting her relax each time. He'd better not do any more until she told him he could, but he didn't need to do any more. He'd got enough of a start.

He felt her fumbling below him to undo his shorts.

She intended even more?

Of course she did. She'd told him that they would make love before they left here, and she intended that it would happen right now.

Well, that would be one way to get everything dry.

Could this be happening to us so soon?

This was too much for one man to experience.

She sat up from him, exposing her breasts fully to him again to hold. Sliding her hands down between their bodies, she unclipped his shorts and took down his zip, eagerly pushing at his shorts and his underwear to get them down his legs as he raised his hips to let her do that before she went for him, already seeing what she was doing to him.

There would be no missing that part of him! Sobering! Very sobering!

He flinched when he felt her touch him and then take decisive hold.

She didn't seem shy to be doing any of this.

Did she need his help to get into her? It didn't seem like it. Except he was too tensed up... too close to 'coming', already.

"You will need to help me, James, please. I've never done this before."

She did need his help. Her panties were already far enough out of his way.

That request, and confession, didn't help his mood. He was rapidly becoming more helpless as well as breathless.

He tried to help, knowing where this could go now; clearing hair delicately along her vulva so that he would have open access to her vagina... when she eventually put him there and let herself down upon him to get him into her, if that was what she intended.

Why did he even question it? It was going to happen, and with a woman he barely knew, but one who'd hit him emotionally like a ton of bricks. He pulled her cheeks apart and helped her as far as he could without hurting her or scaring her... he hoped.

She even got him started into her... partially... as she moved herself above him, rotating her hips, concentrating, focusing.

His reddening face, and his pained expression told her what she needed to know as she pushed him into her to get him started, no matter how tight the space was, or what it cost her in terms of discomfort. Once she'd got him started, she sat up then settled back down on him, moving her hips to trap him there with some of her weight, not letting him escape.

Nothing was going to 'give', easily, to let him into her. It never did, the first time. She was murderously snug on him and it must be uncomfortable for her too.

He kissed her under her ear this time, encouraging her, but she wasn't having any of that distraction just yet. She knew exactly what she wanted. She leaned forward on him as he held her up from him with his hands upon her breasts, and used both hands under herself to try to open herself even more for him, getting him better started, even if just the 'helmet', at first, could get into her.

She concentrated, focusing, almost sobbing in frustration at the difficulty of it, leaving the pressure of her increasing weight upon him to let him slide into her a little more.

Once this process began, there would be no likelihood of it stopping until she'd achieved what she intended and he was fully into her where they both desperately needed him to be.

How could this be happening so soon between them? This wasn't right. Why hadn't he stopped her? Why hadn't she held back? This would not end well for either of them if they were not careful.

She'd got him started. That was all it would take. Now, it was up to him to play his part too. They could both work on it and cooperate from here… a little push, here… a little push there, to send him where he so needed to be. He'd better not slip out of her or she'd need to struggle with it again. This was not something where failure was an option. There was too much at stake for her. For them both.

He gave in. He was only human. The temperature in their little space was already climbing.

"My breasts." She whispered, pleadingly, her eyes flashing playfully.

"Hold my breasts harder. Touch them. The nipples. Caress them. Please."

He could even kiss them if he wanted to. He obliged, as she focused on the other. He sensed how difficult it was for her to let him into her.

She needed to be distracted from the discomfort of it, feeling as though something might tear... but she was determined. She was not the only woman who'd ever faced this problem. There was a first time for everything, and this needed to be put behind them as soon as possible.

He felt an almost painful tightness upon him, threatening to strip his foreskin back, keeping him from making progress to help her. She wasn't backing off. She persisted, moving him millimeter by millimeter into her as she kissed him in an abandoned kind of way, almost throwing her body around in her desperation to battle past all resistance and to get him into her at any cost.

She should have wetted him with her saliva.

Too late now. She had her eyes closed and was focused on what she was doing; also fighting away any hesitation on her part. She seemed doggedly intent not to let this moment pass without moving this to its inevitable conclusion first.

This was her first time for this! It had to be for her to be this tight on him, but she was determined!

Once she'd got him started, he was determined, too. The snag was... he wouldn't be long in coming. She'd been tormenting him for long enough, and he was as hard as iron, unable to help himself, now that he was so close to going into her.

He daren't push to help her, even though every part of him was telling him to just push hard and to get it over with as quickly as possible. *'She'll thank you for it later'*. No, she wouldn't. He would hurt her too much.

He'd better warn her when he was coming, and that he would be pushing especially hard at that moment, though he would try not to just push into her without any consideration. He was still a minute or two away from that... with luck.

He would prefer to be fully into her when he came… if he could get into her, but she was having difficulty. She was definitely a virgin; despite the bold way she'd come onto him. He was her first. He didn't think there were any virgins left, once they got to about thirteen years old.

What the hell had made her decide so quickly that he was going to be her first? And out here of all places, and at this moment?

He knew. He'd wanted her the same way the moment he'd started to help her, so he was glad she'd made the first move.

He focused on kissing her—as she was kissing him—and holding her breasts, letting her decide how fast and how far he'd get into her, but she'd better make it happen soon, or he'd come, ready or not.

Something happened. She seemed to open-up suddenly to him with a cry as she slid down over him, taking them both by surprise. He felt that. She'd done that herself with her letting more of her weight down onto him. That sudden release was a shock to them both.

He couldn't help himself then, but pushed in response to that, to be sure he was all the way in. No half measures allowed at this advanced stage.

She groaned, feeling him slide into her, not stopping him from doing that, or wanting him out of her now. He had to help her then, pushing himself yet again, reflexively, to help, to make sure he was all the way in, and that she couldn't back away.

*She wasn't backing away, and he **was,** all the way in.*

It had been difficult enough, but she had no intention of backing away now, and yes... he *was*... all the way in. He had to be. He pushed again to be sure.

He started to come, almost immediately. There would be no holding back on that. It would be like standing in the way of a galloping horse, and it would be entirely pointless.

Success!

He told her; warned her with some urgency, if she needed warning.

"I'm coming, Louise. I'll probably push hard into you again when that happens."

Too late to worry about that. He was breathless already.

There would be no 'probably' about it. Had he just said that? There would be no doubt, whatsoever, about it. His mind began to close down as the pace picked up and his breathing became more labored.

She knew what was happening to him now, and she would soon find out for herself what it meant when a man 'came', inside of her.

Women knew everything. In their little cabals in the schoolyard, and in the university, they discussed it all in detail, whispering behind their hands, or not caring a damn and blurting it out in your face.

...How many times so and so had done Beryl, that one night.

Six times? The sod! The admirable, brutal sod!

They had been suitably impressed, marveling at it while expressing commiseration and shock. Poor girl hadn't got any sleep before he was wanting at her again with that immense package of his. No arguing with him. There should be a law....

At the same time, they were envious that Beryl had been so well attended.

Then, when he'd dropped her off at the residence that next morning, as though she'd just arrived back from home, where she was supposed to have gone that weekend, didn't he raise her skirt again and do her again in the shadow beside the main door. Only after that little farewell flurry, did he let her go inside, to deal with him running from her, down her leg and into her shoe. She climbed the stairs to her room, hoping no one had seen them, or saw her present discomfort.

He'd given her back her panties at that same moment (she could be thankful for that) and she had them clutched in her hand when she should have been pushing them under her to catch him.

Women were idiots that way.

That moment was when James 'came', with a gasp, and a forceful, catatonic push, followed by others, presaging each pulse of sperm, blasting deep into her body. She even felt something; feeling the extreme emotion expressed in that act of reflexive semi-consciousness. People and animals were at their most vulnerable at that moment when their consciousness of their surroundings contracted down, to become focused entirely within their own bodies and what they were doing at that single moment.

She silently rejoiced. *He was hers, now, for sure!*

He'd raised himself into her, unable to stop himself, pulling at her cheeks, pulling her down hard onto him to get deeper into her, but he was already into her as far as he could go. He couldn't help himself. He'd had to push, always trying to get farther in. It was a natural reflex.

He pushed again, almost desperately, and then pushed again to be sure, groaning and gasping each time.

He'd come too quickly, damn!

His breathing gradually slowed as they kissed, their eyes closed as they recovered from that mad gallop.

They seemed to die, together. This was what 'life' was all about.

James held her still, stroking the back of her head as he held her onto him.

"Are you okay, Louise?" At least he still knew her name.

Now, he was concerned for the damage he'd done to her?

She turned her head to kiss him. "Yes. Of course I am, James."

She seemed pleased... able to forgive him for hurting her. And he *had*, hurt her, but she wouldn't say anything about that.

"What just happened?"

She laughed in disbelief. *Did he really need to ask?*

"If you don't know what happened, James, then we are in serious trouble."

Or he was. She knew there was more behind his question than that.

He tried to clarify. "I asked, not because I don't know what just happened, physically, between us (it was still happening). I do know, but I asked because I am confused over how *quickly* it happened between us; unexpectedly quickly, as wrong as that must have been, and it is going to happen again, very soon… if I may... if it won't hurt you too much."

The damage had been done. Once, or ten times, it wouldn't matter much. What did he mean about it being wrong? It had not been wrong at all, but necessary.

She knew he would do it again, even a few more times before they parted.

"Good. There was nothing wrong in that. We both needed that to happen, or didn't you sense that? And you may do that again, please, whenever you want to. You just have to ask." Or even not bother to ask. "That was... interesting."

That word, 'interesting', covered a lot of meanings.

She seemed to like the idea of him repeating that, rather than of her cursing him for what he'd done. Her eyes were sparkling as she looked down at him.

No woman had ever looked at him like that before.

Where had she been all of his life? He tried asking again.

"What made you take charge and do that wonderful thing for me Louise? That was courageous, and so welcome, as well as being well beyond my wildest expectations."

The whole process had caught him flat footed.

"I did it because I had to do it for you. It was necessary to move us forward before we left here. Do you regret it happening? I don't. It drew us together."

"I would never regret that, but what made you…?" His words trailed off as she looked down at him.

He knew, but he hadn't connected the dots yet.

"I hope you know what happens next, between us, James. What should happen next." He didn't want to think, just yet, but she was making him think, by asking questions.

"More of the same? Yes, please." He was being half serious.

He would always be ready for more.

She chuckled and snuggled into him and kissed him. "I will not mind if you want to."

Could he survive any more of this?

She persisted. "I meant, what happens between us next, following on from that. Further out in time."

He thought about it, seeing what she was getting at. "I think so. We have to discuss where we go from here in a philosophical sense, our lives, our entire futures together."

Now he knew, and he was on the same page as her.

He'd felt it too. That was a relief, that she didn't need to explain everything to him.

She continued. "I see that as the next step, once we get out of here, or even before we leave. At least we both seem to be waking up to the same possibilities that will change everything for us both. I feel as though I have known you forever."

He felt the same way she did. Making love, seemed to do that for a lot of people.

He kissed her then, feeling it returned.

Love. That was what this was all about. There would be no secrets between them now; no holding back.

She seemed to intercept his thoughts.

"I don't think we were slow, or held back in any way, did we, James, once we knew what we wanted?"

She hadn't... that was for sure.

"No. We didn't." His mind was still clouded with emotion and the feelings of what he had just accomplished.

"How did we get to this stage so quickly, as to do this? Two hours ago I didn't even know you existed."

He, was asking her? It would soon come to him when he thought more about it. She, knew, but men were always slow to catch on. It was something to do with the 'little head', confusing the 'big head'. Women didn't have that same problem, but that 'little head' would always be of increasing importance to them as they took increasing possession of it to make it theirs. She found that thought, amusing.

He tried to clarify his question. "When I asked what happened, I wasn't asking about the physical aspect—I know about that, of course (he was repeating himself again)—I was wondering how… we'd both got to this stage together, mentally and emotionally at the same time, for it to happen so quickly, knowing so little of each other? We've only just met." It was all, so confusing for him.

She stroked his ears and caressed his cheek. She seemed more in charge now. They knew enough about each other, and it would grow from here. They had the rest of their lives to think about this.

"I think, James, that if you think about our very first moments together, as we met, it might just come to you."

"You mean, the intoxication we both felt, and this growing feeling of becoming addicted, never wanting to be separated from each other again? This feeling that I'll never get enough of you this way, or any other way?"

She nodded. *He knew! He'd felt it too. He was in love, but like any man he couldn't admit it easily so soon.*

"But it's also even more than that… ethereal, transcendental. We are both in a different world than the one out there. This one, is ours, and ours alone, and one, of our own making."

He thought about it. She made sense. He was in love. She was in love. They were in love with each other.

He'd had no idea when he'd set out this morning that this would be part of his day, and nor had she.

"I guess we do have a lot to talk about now." They had everything to talk about… a lifetime of things.

Her eyes sparkled, seeing the full understanding of it take hold of him.

"Before we talk, James, I think… I feel… that it's going to happen to you again, soon, so why don't you just kiss me, please, and let it happen. We'll talk in a short while, after you recover. I want to savor everything that is about to happen to me and to my body again at this moment... feelings, sensations that I've never known before." She was enjoying this strangely developing relationship.

She laid flat on him again, closing her eyes, sensing what he was doing to her again, down there... pushing at her again... into her... though he'd never left her.

He came again, not quite as eagerly or as easily that time, as the first, and it was gentler. He flopped back, exhausted, beneath her, the perspiration standing out on his forehead as he looked up at her; feeling more of it running off his abdomen. He felt it moving from hair follicle, to hair follicle, like an insect picking its way across his belly. He was still damned hard and would never want to come out of her. Ever. This, where he was in her body, would be his home.

"My sisters will kill me for this. Taking advantage of you so soon."

Where had that thought come from?

No, they wouldn't. Louise would intervene and plead for him.

"My mother will want to kill me too, James... figuratively... for the reckless speed of all of this, but we are both adults. I am not ashamed of what happened, and I know that you are not. Our emotions are honest."

He liked the way she was looking down at him.

"Love." He managed to use the word without making it a question, seeing her nodding, pleased with him for having got it, and being able to say it.

"Love. Love at first sight, for me." She confirmed it.

"For me too, but I was slow to understand what my feelings were telling me." His hormones had got in the way.

So, this was what being in love felt like.

'Love at first sight', or as close to 'first sight', as mattered.

No stuffing that Genie back into the bottle.

'Love at first sight'.

James liked that thought.

"If you kiss me again, it will help me to understand it better, I think. I was captivated by you from that first moment, and I began to have the feeling that this was all fore-ordained, even this morning as I set out, and I didn't even know it."

He slowly pushed into her again, not wanting to leave her, exploring this new sensation, watching her face to be sure he wasn't hurting her now, and that he wasn't dreaming any of it.

Neither had she known that they would meet like this, or could even have dreamed that it might be possible. He wouldn't question it. There were a hundred little side roads on the path of life, and this had been one of them. A road taken, or a road not taken; had he walked in a different direction... had he been earlier or later setting out this morning... had she not sheltered in the lee of that rock... had it not rained.... A person could go mad trying to sort out those thousands of little events coming together exactly as they had... combinations, permutations, and trying to find a guiding force, or a reason, where none existed. Fate.

He tried to get them both comfortable without disturbing anything. How had they both become almost naked with each other so quickly?

It had just... happened... had been needed.

He gave up trying to sort a reason out for any of it. Happenstance. Serendipity. Whatever.

"Thank you, Louise. I've never done that before with any woman. You were my first for this." He had no difficulty admitting it.

Boys usually wanted to give the impression that they were studs, with a retinue of eager, receptive girls lined up behind him waiting to be serviced just by him, and that it was a common everyday thing.

"And you, for me, James. Thank you. You were gentle (she was being kind and forgiving. He hadn't been gentle. Nothing about this would ever be gentle at first). Though it was exceptionally forceful at the end, and you took me by surprise."

They'd taken each other by surprise.

He touched her gently by the face. "As long as I didn't hurt you too much."

He'd probably hurt her when he'd lanced into her unexpectedly… and then, when he'd come…! That would have surprised her too. The sheer force of it had surprised even him. He wanted to feel that sensation again, and as often and as soon as possible, never wanting to come out of her, but his own body would dictate that.

"What made you decide to do that for me, Louise? That was a big step for you." He thought of something else. "I must be hurting you. Do you want me to come out of you?"

That was a strange question to be asking anyone, but they would have a lot of similar, personal things to say to each other when they continued this, as they would, and even before they left here.

She hadn't done it just for him. She'd done it for herself too. It had been necessary.

"No. Don't leave me yet, don't come out of me. There's no point in retreating now. It feels strange, having all of you, all of that, inside me, but it was needed between us. I need to get used to this feeling of being stretched, and full… and of you being deep inside me."

It would happen often, now.

"I knew what I wanted to have happen between us, almost as soon as you helped me, when you stood over me even, and wanted to help."

She blushed. "You were aroused even then. I couldn't help but notice (a woman noticed that), but you weren't too threatening. I suppose I was aroused too; not understanding it at first, breathless, not sure why I felt as I did, but women respond differently. I didn't want to lose you, so I did what I thought would help to hold you close to me. That's why I needed to do this with you."

He kissed her. "You wouldn't have lost me. I wouldn't have let you out of my sight after meeting you as I did." He kissed her again as he assured her of that.

She knew that now. So, she hadn't really needed to do what she'd done, but she didn't regret doing it.

She confessed even more. "I need to think about this, now that I can, and try and understand how it happened between us so fast. How I intended it would happen the way it did. Because I did intend it. I saw what you were feeling… how excited you were… how difficult it was for you to suggest that 'some' of my clothes should come off. It sounded so daringly improper and quite took my breath away."

She laughed at that thought. "You expected me to object, but I was too wet and cold to argue. As we progressed and I saw how embarrassed you were and how shy, I lost all of my concerns and fear. You can blame me, if you need to. A moral woman would never have done that, but I didn't want to be moral. I wanted you, to want me. I know it was wrong… but…."

He stopped her. "It wasn't wrong, Louise. Not between, us. As you said, it was necessary."

He was as much to blame for what had happened, being aroused the whole time he'd helped her, undressing her, and unable to do anything about it to control himself, but also not taking advantage of her too much.

She'd detected that about him and had not objected as her clothes progressively came off. She should have been more cautious.

Hell! She'd been cautious her whole life. If she expected her life to change, then she had to change it. So, she had. And how!

He kissed her. "I wanted it to happen too, even as soon as I met you, but what could I do or say that wouldn't have had you panicking? Men are not at all subtle. We get too obvious in so many ways." Especially with that weapon of theirs when their emotions took over their brain.

She'd noticed.

"You got to me." He seemed to feel about her, as she felt about him. That made her feel so much better about that. Her mother would be shocked. She'd have to tell her some of this, eventually… about how they'd met, but not all of it.

Now, they really *did*, have a lot to speak about.

They laid there for a long time, still learning more about each other; kissing, holding, touching; wanting this to keep going.

The way he felt, he wouldn't be long in coming again. He would be able to talk to her about that, as he did that, and about so many other things that a woman would never otherwise know.

At least they wouldn't lose track of each other after this, no matter where they were.

I would like to know more.

They talked, learning more about each other; exchanging a lifetime of experiences that needed to be touched upon in the space of the next hour or so, until they would need to leave here.

There were so many things they didn't know about each other, so they would slowly have to fill in those gaps.

"We were both at the same university, yet we didn't know about each other until now. We will be living in the same city too. Whereabouts in Manchester do you live James?" She needed to know, and she should know. They would be living together.

He explained. "I live with an older couple in a relatively large house, not so far out; just back from the ring road, the freeway. They were my first lodgings when I started university, and within walking distance of the college."

He mentioned the estate. It was a good thirty minutes' walk to the university. He seemed to like walking. But of course he did, to be up here.

She began to be excited. "I'll be teaching in that part of the city too. I start a teaching job in two weeks at the girls' high school there; Burnham college for girls, and I'll need to find somewhere to live before then." She'd planned on going there to find lodgings before term began, but it seemed that it was already being taken care of.

He laughed softly, and touched her face. "Fate smiles on us again, my love. I know the school. I'm no more than a ten-minute walk from there too. That clinches it then. You will live with me."

He would have to clear it with the older couple he lived with, but he knew there would be little problem there.

She would live with him… there would never be any other possibility now, and it was all being so easily solved without her lifting a finger. She liked where this was going.

"I will be buying that house." This sounded strange.

"Why? That takes time, buying a house. What if it's not for sale?"

He had a ready answer to everything.

"It's for sale to me. The older couple; the Finnings, that I live with, have a big old house in a good neighborhood behind that school.

They'd let if run down over the years because of their age. I asked their permission to do a few things and they were surprised, not expecting that. So, in my spare moments and at weekends, I became their gardener and general repair man. I did the roofing (a few tiles), plumbing (stopping a few leaks), carpentry (sticking doors), electrical… masonry work; whatever needed to be done.

"They let me live in the converted carriage house at the end of the property, for a nominal rent."

He explained more of the circumstance.

"They weren't able to do everything they needed to get done, to the house themselves, and contractors were too ready to take advantage of them, so I offered to work on the weekends and in other moments of spare time. An hour here, an hour there. That was three years ago. They gradually adopted me in so many ways. I even look after their house when they go to Spain in winter."

She was happy to learn whatever she could.

"They have no children of their own, so they offered to sell me the house if I wanted it. Part of the deal would be that I would allow them to live out their lives there. I didn't mind. I was already independent of them, living in the old Carriage house, and it would be a wonderful arrangement as far as I was concerned. It all depended on if I decided to put roots down in Manchester, and I hadn't decided about that until now."

But now he had? She liked to hear that.

"They offered it to me at a good price, since I'd grown attached to it, and to them. I still have a few years to finish, and to decide, so I hesitated, until now, not sure what my plans were. But not anymore. They'll be pleased to hear that. I can easily get a job in the city.

"They even let my sisters visit and help too, in exchange for staying with me. We are a blended family, I suppose. We, you and I, will live there, if you will not object, if I am not moving too fast for you."

Moving too fast? They were moving fast... look at what they were already doing with each other, but there was nothing wrong with it. They knew they were in love and that they wanted to be together from here to eternity.

"They'll be pleased to meet you."

Except they wouldn't be married. That might be some time away, and that might cause some difficulties.

"I'll introduce you as my wife, as unofficial as that will be, and explain a few things about that; how suddenly we met, and how we knew about each other almost immediately; how it's just a matter of time before we do, actually marry. They'll understand."

They might not.

"Are we moving too fast, James?"

"Undoubtedly, we are, but life is too short to waste any of it. That's what they keep telling me, and I know it for myself now."

He hesitated.

"There is just one problem."

She waited.

"How do we tell your parents about this? This is far too sudden. They won't like this!" His parents might have something to say too.

She put a finger over his lips.

"I'll think of something." They didn't have to approve.

Other things were happening between them again.

"I think you are growing in me and getting that way again, James." He certainly was. Their conversation and their physical closeness and touching, kept bringing him to life.

He moved to make them more comfortable as she pushed her damp shorts behind him to protect his back from the hard rock as he pushed up into her once more.

"I'll come again, soon. You excite me in ways I didn't think were possible."

She liked to hear that. How was he able to do this so many times? Yet Trevor, her elder brother was doing this to Marjorie, his lifelong girlfriend. Marjorie had told her that once Trevor had started doing her, when they'd been only fourteen, that was all he seemed to think of, and that they had so many little places they could escape to and make love. The entire village knew, and was even keeping count. They'd even been observed in the old sand pit, with bets being made as to how many times he'd do her, before they moved on to the next place.

James had to stop talking and focus again on what they were doing to each other. It was a good thing that he hadn't come out of her.

After everything had quieted down again, with them both breathing heavily, she laid on him for a few more minutes, and then let him know how she was feeling now.

"I'm uncomfortable. I need to pee, James, so you'll have to come out of me."

He needed to pee too, but he'd been holding off, not wanting to come out of her so soon, and to lose this incredible sensation she gave him.

"How should I do this? I don't want to go out there to get wet and cold again."

"You won't. You don't have to. After I come out of you, you can move down to position yourself between my knees, as you continue to lie on me. They'll hold you off the ground. You can pee between my legs onto the ground."

She blushed and smiled. "It could get messy. I splash."

He laughed. "I'm not worried. The rain will soon solve that when we leave here. It will wash our legs off. I've never done this before either."

There had been a lot of, 'firsts'.

She raised herself cautiously from him, feeling him leave her body slowly, watching him come out of her with an audible gasp from him as he dropped from her. He hadn't liked that feeling. He was still big and still quite solidly hard, but was also wet, from her. They could get back to that again when she'd finished.

He moved her clothing higher onto her back, and then struggled to ease her panties off her, as well as taking off his own shorts and undewear (down near his ankles by then) as she stayed close to him for his warmth.

She laid upon him, down near his knees; his not-so-obvious phallus (but still damned impressively big and firm) pushing up into her, between her breasts as he held her off the ground.

He wanted to help her pee, but knew that he couldn't.

He heard her; saw the warm vapor from her urine rising into the cooler air… could smell her, bringing him back to life for her again. She'd notice that, considering where he was, between her breasts.

She wasn't long.

She was also losing his sperm, too, feeling some discomfort as he leaked from her vagina, and down her vulva. Her vagina felt strange; quite different from what it usually did, having been well-used several times now. She would need to stay like this for a minute or two, still getting rid of him.

He reached out to touch her after she'd peed. She was still open to him, letting him feel where he had just been in her, and how receptive for him she still was and would always be. There was some of him leaking out of her, and a thin smudge of blood on his fingers when he looked.

He helped her back up on him.

"You were losing me from you as you peed, and there is a suggestion of some blood. Are you sure I didn't hurt you when I pushed into you?"

She used her panties to dab at herself to dry off, looking at them for herself. Maybe there was a faint hint of blood.

"Not enough to matter, James. And I will correct you. *You*, didn't push into *me*. I pushed down onto you, as you helped. I had to do that to get this started properly between us, and to get it over with. All it took was determination. It didn't hurt too much, and then it was over with. I'll never be a virgin again, that's for sure, and glad to be rid of it, to you."

They both smiled.

"Your turn to pee now."

She moved to be close beside him to let him pee in turn, her arms over him, and watched. He turned away from her, holding himself, closing his eyes as he focused. She couldn't help him with this, and she shouldn't distract him. He was still partially aroused, and that, in his hand, was hers now… all of it, whenever she wanted it.

He was still leaking slowly from her. She could feel that.

It took him a minute of concentration to become relaxed enough to pee, but stopping and starting, as though it pained him, before he was able to continue in a steady stream. It would soon drain away.

After he'd peed, she reached over and held him tenderly in her hand as she asked him about this part of his, able now to give in to her curiosity in a way she never could have before.

"He's a little softer now, I think."

He smiled. "We both are. A pair of real softies"

She could now ask questions about this, feeling him still changing as she held him and talked, learning what she could, bringing him back to life without even trying to.

He would soon be ready for her again. He was still stiff enough to go back into her.

He turned back to her and helped her above him again, going into her once more as though he'd never left her, feeling her slowly settle fully onto him again as he covered her with their clothing once more to keep her warm. They laid there again, marveling at this, that was happening to them yet again.

He heard the rain still coming down.

He adjusted their position together to make it easier on them both.

They would soon need to leave. The weather wasn't going to let up. She was warmer than she had been, and her clothes were drier than a couple of hours earlier.

We need to leave here.

The day was advancing. They needed to get dressed, and to leave here, but they'd never forget this place where everything had changed so unexpectedly for them, bringing them together so intimately, and so decisively.

They'd even bring their children up here, pointing out to them where they'd first met in a storm, but not telling them all of the wonderful details after that. There would be children, but not too soon and not just yet.

"We should get dressed, and get you home. I'll get you down safely. You can have some of my drier clothes and this poncho, and I'll wear whatever of yours will fit me."

It was difficult to conduct a conversation while they were still locked together as they were, and always on the cusp of losing control and finding themselves heading down that inescapable slope of climaxing again. At least their conversation was marginally distracting.

He could still hear the rain drumming upon their flimsy cover, with the wind constantly trying to take if off them.

"I'll get wet, but I can tolerate that for an hour or two where you can't." She didn't need to get wet and miserable again, but this, what they were doing, more than made up for that initial misery.

She listened, knowing that them getting ready to leave here was not open for argument, but she could tell him a few things.

"It will take us about two hours to get down to my home. You are likely to get wet, James." He liked the way she looked at him and used his name.

"I'll survive." They would, now that they had each other.

"We'll have to help each other. You can have a hot bath at home, and you'll be staying the night." She was very sure about that. The way she said it was also full of promise of other things.

He laughed, but it was not a humorous laugh.

"Your parents will have something to say about that." All parents would. She couldn't just drag a strange man into the house to meet them and then calmly dictate terms like that. Not even in this weather.

She shook her head in denial of his doubting her.

"Maybe. Once… they might have had a lot to say about what I did with my life, but not now. I'm of age to make my own decisions. I'm a big girl. If I have to, I'll remind them of that."

*She **was** a big girl, and in all of the right ways, and places. He'd discovered that for himself. He was still discovering that. Thank god she'd had the courage to continue what he'd had no choice in getting started.*

He continued to see difficulties for them.

"They'll know all about me the moment they lay eyes on me, and when they see you." He was too obviously plundering their daughter. One look at their faces would tell them everything. She was no longer as innocent as she had been, setting out that morning.

He was trying to warn her of what his reception was likely to be like when they entered her home, dressed as they would be, and having exchanged so many clothes. They'd want him out of their lives just as fast as he'd come into them.

"I expect so, but they'll understand when they see how wet you are, and I tell them how you helped me. I'll tell them you saved my life, because you did." He wasn't sure that was true, but it might be. She would even tell them she loved him, and that they were in love. That would make them think twice.

She'd better not tell them too much.

"I have two brothers who…" *who, what?...* "but they won't be a problem for you. I know some of their secrets, so they'd better behave themselves."

Four against two. They were good odds, the way he was feeling.

He would tackle anything for this woman; even irate brothers after his balls.

"Mom is the ruling force in our family, but Dad doesn't mind. He likes it better that way. 'Happy wife, happy life', he says. They love each other."

Of course they did. They loved their daughter too. They didn't know *him*.

"They'll see right through me."

"And me too, James. I've never brought anyone home before. I never had time for boys. Until now. They'll be surprised."

Surprised, would be the understatement of the year. *A tornado ripping into and through their daughter's life, as well as her body, removing her clothes and replacing them with his. It would be too bloody obvious how things had gone, along with their daughter's virginity.*

"I'll tell them how it is."

She should be careful.

"You'll be staying and, somehow… you'll be with me tonight." She sounded determined about that. She was opening up a lot of trouble for them both.

"They might try to stop me, but I'll tell them how it will be, and that we will be living together in Manchester anyway when I get there, so that's settled. They can't stop us. I'm old enough to decide my own future and I am within a week or two of leaving home anyway."

They'd still object.

She'd already made up her mind, and he knew better than to argue with any woman, especially one he was in love with, but he could see what would happen. He'd be lucky to escape with his life!

He kissed her, rather than argue. "Let's get you dressed and get out of here." He needed her to know something else.

"However, you should stay exactly where you are for the moment…." She knew where that was. "I might be able to… I can pretty well guarantee…." She knew. He would soon come again.

He would dress as much of her as he could with her sitting on him like that. He would be able to come again. She could help him there.

She should keep count of how many times that would be.

"I'll dress you, and then you can dress me, but let's not rush it, and be ready to stop when I…." When he reached another climax in her.

She kissed him as he held her breasts, giving him permission to do anything else he wanted.

"Bra, first." It might be a close run race; getting her dressed or giving in again.

She sat up from him as she looked knowingly down into his face, sending him deeper into her.

He groaned and tried to focus as he slid her bra straps up her arms, loath to hide such perfection away, adjusting them for her to get the cups exactly positioned upon them, changing his mind. He needed one more look at them, and to kiss them and touch them again before he hid them completely away, but still coming back to adjust and to check on them. He would never be able to leave them alone.

She would wear his shirt and sweater. They were still drier than hers. Hers, would fit him and they would dry on him as they walked. Maybe, but doubtful.

His shirt and sweater followed that.

Her moving around on him as he'd dressed her, had brought him along again. He closed his eyes and pleaded for a time-out.

"Give me a moment."

She heard the strangled tone of his voice and felt what was happening between them again, staying still, upon him as she watched his face and the wondrous torture of what was taking place for him, pass across it. She stayed motionless, as far as she could, sensing what was happening within her body once again, until his eyes opened, and his breathing slowed again, ending with a heartfelt sigh. That climax had been even gentler than before but he was still breathing hard.

"Thank you, again." He didn't need to thank her. She kissed him.

"Thank, **you**, James."

He picked up dressing her where he'd left off.

"Panties next. I'll have to let you come off me first, but be careful when you do that, or I'll be all over your socks and your clothes, and believe me, you don't want that." It would also be a painful sensation, as he'd discovered, coming out of her too quickly when he least wanted to.

She lifted herself up from him, letting what immediately began to run from her, dribble down his shaft, and onto his belly and into that hair on him there, as they both watched. He was getting his own, back.

He wiped at her with her panties as she leaned over him, with him holding them there between her legs for a few moments. His face was flushed. Her face was flushed too.

She'd better remember to wash her panties out for herself when she got home. Her mother shouldn't see these.

"How should we do this?"

"Turn, and sit on me, higher up, and I'll get them started over your feet. You can have my underwear too, if that won't disgust you."

She looked at him.

"Nothing of yours will ever disgust me, James. Not after what we just did."

"Good. Then I'll put your own shorts back on you. They wouldn't fit me anyway." Her mother would certainly notice that, and might take the broom to him.

Somehow, they managed to dress each other under that poncho, as they prepared to leave. Her pack would go into his.

He would carry those to help keep his back dry, while she would wear his poncho, once he'd put a belt, loosely around it inside the loops to hold it down on her body.

He would find it a miserable walk back to where she lived. Except she would be with him, and that would make up for everything else.

Her presence, needing his help, would take his mind off the weather, and she could help him in other ways. They could stop from time to time to get warmed up again as they made love once more. She would want to reward him for everything he was doing for her. There were lots of sheltered places where they could lie down in that poncho together, with a few of those 'adjustments'.

They'd know when that time came, just by looking at each other. He would always want to make love to her. This was the start of a new life for them both.

At least they could hold hands. He could push his hand into an opening at the side of his slicker as they walked, and they could talk, to take their minds off the discomfort of the weather; learn about each other as they walked, and to make their plans to be together after this. If she had her way, they would never be separated again.

He'd be wet by the time they got to her house, but that didn't matter.

He could take his mind off the rain and his increasing discomfort, by thinking about what she'd told him of her family and of her teaching plans.

It would be interesting to meet her family, except they would see through him in an instant; seeing the way they looked at each other, itching to hold hands again, even to kiss and touch, as well as always wanting to do so much more, now that they knew their feelings for each other. There would never be enough privacy.

Her parents and brothers would undoubtedly see that he'd got too close to their daughter, and sister; that he'd got to know her in that biblical sense. They would want to kill him. Parents with daughters to protect, always did.

He wouldn't blame them. He'd want to kill him too, in their position.

Home.

They stopped twice on the way down, sheltering together under his poncho, resting, as they got warm again.

They ate the rest of his lunch, the first time, kissing and touching, their legs nestling together for warmth, feeding each other, secure in their new-found love. They soon gave in to the real reason they were stopping, loosening their clothing (words were no longer necessary for this expression of love), moving it out of their way to make love again, but doing it slowly this time, learning even more about each other; amazed at how quickly they had grown together in such a revolutionary way.

It was better cushioned here, lying on a bed of bracken that he'd bent over for them before they'd lain down.

The beginning might have been slow, but the ending of it wasn't. Everything he did amazed her. Everything he was learning about her, blew his mind away.

She didn't bother putting her panties on, or his underwear or shorts, after that, knowing that they would soon need to come off again when they stopped for a repeat performance, in about another hour. Besides, it would allow her to get rid of him from her body before they set out again, rather than have it caught by her clothes. Evidence, best not seen too obviously.

She would let him carry her panties for her and let the rain wash them out. It would help him too, in an obvious way, to be holding something so intimate of hers. His underwear and her shorts could be in his backpack to stay dry.

She blushingly told him why she'd left them off—just for him, and their next time—letting that thought work on him, to burrow into his fevered mind. knowing how it would affect him, keeping him alive that special way, for her.

His sweater and shirt were long enough to keep her warm, even if it was drafty, most of the time. At least she was staying dry, even as *he,* got soaking wet. She was concerned for him and let him know it, but all he did was laugh, and kiss her. He had a young body with good energy reserves and was fired up with love.

She dared to reach out to touch him now... amazed at her boldness... wishing that he could leave his shorts off too... telling him what she would most like.

If he did that, or even if he just left them open without his underwear holding him in, she would be able to see him walking with that incredible erection (all of it for her) standing out from his body as she marveled at it, and at him.

It was just for her. All of it, just for her.

It announced to the world around them, that he was that way because of her—this woman he was in love with—but it was maybe too cold for that, so she wouldn't suggest it… this time.

There was a lot of summer left ahead of them. They would do it together again, soon...up here… wander the fells naked, constantly stopping to make love. It was well off the tourist track. No one would see them, and the locals rarely came up here.

He pushed his hand into the poncho through that opening at the side, checking on her, behind her, discovering her mischievously between her legs as she danced and squealed; objecting, while not objecting as he stopped her falling over; feeling her relax onto his hand, letting him touch and discover her again. She was never sure what he would do next, and it kept her attentive to where he was and what he might want.

He'd always want to do that, the devil!

The second time they stopped, they just snuggled under his poncho and went at it again with nothing to get in their way.

When they'd finished, she could see the wraiths of water vapor rising from his damp shoulders. He was tolerating the weather much better than she would have done, but they were also at a much lower elevation, so it was warmer and even out of most of the wind. He was getting a lot of special exercise too. The weather wasn't getting to him as much as it had affected her.

She decided that she would let him put her panties and shorts on her just before they got home, in another half hour, aware that they might need to stop to make love yet again. He would eagerly help her with that, would always be ready for her; soon brought to life. That way, she might not have to wash her panties out as soon as she got home to hide what had happened to her each time they'd stopped.

Her mother would guess, however, and there would be unspoken questions, and others asked directly, if her mother could get her alone. Her mother seemed able to see into the minds of each of her children. She knew their innermost secrets almost as soon as they did. Except there were *some secrets*, she didn't seem to know just yet. Especially about her elder brother, Trevor. David had secrets too, but not nearly as personal as Trevor's--or her own, now. But that would be a secret only until they got home. They would be too obvious, regardless of what they did to stay apart, but they couldn't help that.

James might give the game away by blushing, and by his lack of control of his body when he came close to her, always wanting her that way. Her mother would notice that, for sure, and how she held his hand as she led him into the house, not daring to let him go... as she tried to shield his eagerness for her from view, but he wasn't the kind of man who would run away in panic.

He knew what his reception was likely to be: guardedly cool. Mothers with nubile daughters, always looked at the men their daughters brought home, that way, as though they'd already desecrated their loved ones (often, they had), and that he was walking into the house with unspeakable unpleasantries all over the bottom of his shoes, and others in his mind, just waiting for another opportunity to be at her daughter.

Yes, it would be that obvious.

As they walked up to her house, he felt a slight lurch... had he...? Then he remembered that he'd helped Louise put her wet panties and shorts on, along with his underwear, just five minutes away as they'd played, and kissed; going into her again as he would always want to, but not coming... not quite... but close to it, knowing that it would become difficult for them to be so open with each other once they got inside the house and came under scrutiny.

Difficult? It would be impossible!

Mrs. Prescott had been flying around the kitchen as they'd walked in, obviously busy, but also relieved to see her daughter. However, she was not so relieved to see him with her. Mothers never were. She had a lot of questions, but they would have to wait.

She paused, seeing her daughter dressed in an oilskin that she'd not worn going out, and with a young man in tow behind her. A stranger. A stranger who was too familiar with her daughter in a special way.

He was wet, dripping water everywhere, but he didn't look cold; just exceptionally wet.

"Another ten minutes and I would have been calling out a search party." She didn't hesitate, taking charge immediately.

"Get those outer things off in the porch where they won't do any damage. They can go into the wash." She knew what to say and do. This was still her home, and she ruled it.

That other, could be hung up to drip, outside.

Her eyes flickered over him, but she kept her thoughts to herself.

Too bloody handsome and virile by far. Too attentive to Louise.

This was one of those moments every mother dreaded, or could be pleased about, but she would always need warning, and there had been none.

"Mom, I want you to meet, James."

At least he had a name, unlike most mongrel curs. He'd raped her daughter! He had to have done, yet she didn't seem distressed.

Her mother nodded to him and held her hand out politely. His hand was warm, big, and firm. Just like another part of him already was, for her daughter. She blushed at that thought. She knew about boys. Except this one was a man, and confident of himself, and of her daughter. Even worse!

He was wearing some of the clothes her daughter had gone out with that morning; sweater, and shirt, and she was wearing other clothes; his. They must have had a rare old time with that transfer, but she couldn't ask, and shouldn't even think about it. Wonder of wonders... at least her daughter still had a bra on, but her lips showed signs of puffiness, and she seemed agitated, maybe sore... down there.

There was something going on here, but she didn't have time to ask questions, and to learn what it was, though she felt she knew. Louise was at that age where a man would impact her life (and about time). Though she would have reservations about that ambivalence.

At least he wasn't a local.

"James." She took his hand. "You're not the usual thing she drags home with her from her walks."

No, he was something much worse!

She made her comment sound not-quite-complimentary to him. He seemed to rank lower than a toad or a snake, which she was used to her daughter bringing home, along with other flotsam and jetsom.

Her mother could see that Louise was on edge, wondering what else she would say.

Her daughter was going to be defensive of him, so she stepped back from him and decided to watch what she said, as she continued speaking from the kitchen.

He didn't seem too bad, but she'd reserve judgment. All young men were a threat to any woman like her daughter, except.... She didn't want to think about that change.

"You're soaked through to the skin. Louise will run you a bath and dig out towels, and a change of her brother's clothes for you while I'm out. They seem to fit you (so she had noticed), then she can get those clothes into the washer and dryer."

Keep the beggars busy. She wished she hadn't suggested a bath, but what else could she say?

She looked specifically at her daughter, wordlessly asking her what she was doing, bringing a man home like this, but saying nothing. She watched them both get out of more of their clothes, struggling with their boots--him, helping her, his head touching her legs-- leaving the worst of their wet things in the porch, though her daughter was a lot dryer than he was.

...there was a tale to be told.

She also glimpsed more clothing on, under Louis's shorts than she'd gone out with. His clothing too, no doubt. There was a tale indeed....

She'd have to ask about that too, but later.

He reached out to Louise to steady her as she lost her balance, touching her... holding her close. Too close on her thighs, and too familiar, as they smiled at each other. Too much was being wordlessly said. She ignored that.

Of all the times for her to be going out of the house to pick up her husband and sons!

This was one time she would rather have stayed home and watched what would be going on under her nose after she'd gone; stopping it only temporarily by her presence. She could see what was likely to happen.

They were too obvious in every way! Especially, him.

Surely it was too soon for that?

That plaintive cry was the heartfelt plea of every mother.

The younger generation! They had no restraint.

She had no choice about going.

"I've got dinner started. There's enough for all of us, so don't feel that you need to rush off anywhere in this weather (even if he could, and even if her daughter would have let him). They needed to find out who he was. I have to go and pick up your father and brothers from the station in this downpour with them missing the bus, and I've already lost some time waiting for you to get home. I shouldn't be any more than an hour."

"Sorry I was late, Mom. I'll look after everything here and set the table. I should also phone and let Mrs. Abernethy know that James is here, and is not lost on the fell, somewhere."

Good, keep yourself busy. No doubt she'd find some way to make sure he stayed here tonight. It had already gone too far between them.

So, who'd found who? He was staying at the Inn on the other side of the fell. He was a long way from home. No getting back there, tonight.

Why had she dragged him back here?

It was too obvious. She didn't want to think about it.

It was way too soon for that! Though it had to happen sooner or later, and he didn't look too bad of a rogue... though he had interfered with her daughter in the worst way.

She'd get it all out of them after she got back. Or as much as she could... or dared... or wanted to know.

"Yes, dear. I know you will. There's hot water enough, and everything's cooking. I put the potatoes in the oven over twenty minutes ago, so check them before you take them out. There's hot water for a tea. He looks like he could use a hot drink." They both could.

She kissed her daughter on the cheek; looked steadily at her in a certain way for a full five seconds, asking her so much... *why is he here like this, with you, and wearing your clothes? Why are you wearing his? How did you manage that? Who is he? Where did he come from?...* as though to warn her about something...'Did he...?   But she said nothing, turning away, picking up her keys and her coat.

Of all the times...!

She sighed in resignation. If she couldn't trust her daughter now, she never would. It was too late anyway from what she'd seen. They were both in a deep state of lust.

It brought back too many memories. He was already getting aroused again at the prospect of them being left alone together.

"Don't let dinner burn."

And don't let him distract you with that... that.... What all males tried to get into you before you knew it.

Too late for that too. It would take them all of about two minutes (if that), to get all of their clothes off, and there was nothing she could do about it.

Then she was gone, afraid of what else she would learn when she got back, and what else would have happened between them.

When the Cat's away...

Louise watched her mother drive away, before she turned to James.

They had an hour alone, perhaps a bit more than an hour, and they still had a lot to learn about each other.

"There's no one to see you, or us now, James."

Her next words didn't surprise him too much. "You, we, can leave *all* of our clothes down here, and finish what we started out there just before we got back here."

Her eyes were sparkling again with knowledge of what could now happen yet again, but in a more relaxed and leisurely way, and she had a mischievous smile on her face. She emphasized that word, 'all'.

"Then I'll take you up and run a bath for you."

And what else?

Continue with more of the same.

She had a lot more in mind for him than just that, but mostly with what he could do for her. She wanted to feel him holding her breasts, hypnotized by them, marveling at them, as she marveled in turn about how they interested him... to feel him going into her body again as he overwhelmed her and kissed her. But then she was also interest in learning more of the finer details about him, and that… part, that she'd just been introduced to.

He wasn't going to argue with her, but he wasn't going to be the only one naked either.

Her mother wouldn't come back for at least an hour or more, so they had enough time, provided they didn't waste it.

"I'll start the wash, soon."

They began to undress each other, chuckling, undressing clumsily, and with some eagerness, knowing what would also happen in that time her mother would be away. They dropped everything right there as it came off and stood naked together. Neither of them was shy now.

She moved into him; seeing, feeling that he was ready for her again; wanting to be into her. That much was blindingly obvious. It took her breath away, seeing him for the first time fully naked, standing up and out; more than ready for her. It was enough to leave her breathless and fighting for air.

And that, all of that, had been into her body, and would soon be there again. She'd felt it several times now. The next time wouldn't be any different, but it would be easier.

He'd never seen her fully naked like this, either, and he liked what he was seeing. She was magnificent in every way, proud, confident, with her perfectly symmetrical breasts, a small patch of hair that did little to hide much of her there (he would soon be nestled in there again), and gorgeous, broad hips that he wanted to touch and feel for himself as he went into her body.

If he wasn't careful, he'd 'come', just thinking about it.

Her ears were burning, and she must be blushing. He was watching her face as he reached out and touched her breasts—hesitantly at first, as though for the first time—then covering them with his entire hands as she pushed into them.

He must know what she was thinking and how she was feeling.

Their socks were the last things to come off them both. He knelt in front of her, pulling her toward him as she held his head close into her in turn. She raised each leg in turn, to his shoulder as he requested, to get the sock off slowly as he inspected what was opened up to him again as she did that, touching gently up into her with his other hand while pushing his face into her as she moved forward over him with his hand pulling at her, behind her.

He slowly fell back onto their pile of clothes, pulling her down with him, to straddle over his face.

She felt him kissing her where no man had ever kissed before as she settled onto his face, and doing other things to her there too.

She'd heard of a man wanting to kiss a woman there, but she wasn't sure it would ever happen to her. It felt strange, but exciting, setting other things flowing along.

After some moments of that, he stood up from her and brought her to her feet as they came together once more, even ferociously this time; kissing, holding firmly, touching, discovering.

She wasn't as concerned by his size and eagerness to have her now, as she had been the first time. Truth to tell, she hadn't been so concerned even then. It just had to happen.

He was touching her breasts—always would want to be touching them—holding them as they kissed.

He needed more.

She moved closer to him and let him see that she wanted him into her; putting him between her legs, helping him find her.

It was different this way, standing up. She had to learn these different ways of them making love, so this would be a good start.

She went onto her tip toes, with him lifting and pulling at her cheeks to get into her as she helped him where she could, pushing his tip up and into her with her finger ends reaching behind herself to get him started into her. She rotated her hips to help him do that, having only a little difficulty getting him into her now.

He held her leg up near his waist with his hand sliding along it under her as he pushed, sliding steadily into her, feeling where he was, in her, with his finger ends touching both himself... his shaft... and into that hair of hers as he progressed to her inner labia, pulling them gently apart.

They almost unbalanced in their eagerness and fell over, chuckling about that.

Everything about her was exciting.

They almost lost their balance again as he adjusted their position together, with him already beginning to breath more noticeably.

He was coming, already?

He was indeed, even though his mind screamed in objection.

He pushed, groaned, and then froze, before pushing hard again. He was out of breath already, and was kissing her as though he'd never kissed her before.

She even felt him coming this time, feeling him lifting her bodily upon him with that item alone as he pushed again, and again; hard enough to shake her fillings loose.

She wanted to laugh at first, but instead, cried out softly at the surprise and the force of it all, but she choked even that back, deciding to stay silent if she could, and not distract him.

Nothing, would distract him at this point.

He slowly climbed down from that cloud he was on, letting her down to stand on the floor again as he slowly retreated from her body with a gasp. He stood, lost for a moment, like the stallion she had once seen by accident, when his gigantic member had dropped from the mare to hang limply beneath him. He had been spent, exhausted, (but not for long), soon reviving to continue. She'd retreated fast from that deeply disturbing scene, her thoughts utterly confused.

James was looking at her, kissing her again as he gently touched her where he'd just been. She was even more moist now, and she was still open to him, where'd he'd been, and soon would be again.

She felt him running out of her, down her leg to the floor!

She swore, snatched up her panties and pushed them into her to catch what she could, holding them there by clenching her legs together on them.

They would go into the wash first, so she wouldn't worry about leaving any traces of what they had done. She would check the flagstone floor, later. It wouldn't do for anyone to slip on what she'd lost.

"You are a naughty boy, James."

He grinned at her and nodded.

"I will always want to be naughty, with you."

She picked up his underwear too, and slowly wiped them over him as she held him tenderly, learning about his testicles, cushioning them, leaning in to kiss him there on the end of it, to thank him for coming into her life, and coming into her, and coming, and coming, and coming. He was salty, and glistening wet from being in her body, and he was still leaking from his tip. She would need to ask about that, and a lot of even more specific things.

They had covered something about this in biology, but nothing specific to a rampant male human. They'd watched mice copulating, but that had been no preparation for this, and tame and unexciting by comparison.

One day she would collect some of that and look at it under the microscope, seeing those thousands of wriggling spermatozoa. His. They were also swimming around in her body too, but they were destined not to achieve anything.

It was a strange thought, there being so many hundreds of thousands of them that she couldn't feel, battling to get beyond her cervix.

They wouldn't do any damage to her yet. It was the wrong time of month for that, and there was no ovum to meet them.

They'd need to talk about that too, before she got pregnant.

He may have come out of her too soon to be leaking like that. He could go back into her if he wanted to.

This was all too funny, and yet it was also too serious for mere words to express.

They had even more to talk about now, but bathing was more important. She glanced at the clock.

"The sweaters will have to go into a cold wash, but I'll get these other things going."

He picked up the clothes he'd dropped and followed her, with hers, mesmerized by what he could see of her as she moved gracefully into the kitchen ahead of him, and then beyond it to the laundry. Her breasts were moving in a way that totally held his attention, if he wasn't looking at her cheeks and hips. He would have reached out to touch, but for the clothes he was carrying.

She got it started on a warm wash as he watched, then dropped some detergent into it.

He was still mesmerized by what he could see of her as she leaned over to look into the washer.

He wanted to help, except that would startle her if he came too close to her, the way he was, and with what he wanted to do to her as he wrapped his arms around her.

Those clothes would be ready to go into the dryer in another hour; by the time her mother got back, but they would both be dressed again by then, with all evidence of what they'd done to each other, long tidied away.

She took his hand as he followed her upstairs. He couldn't help himself, touching up at her with his other hand as she climbed ahead of him, causing her to squeal in her sudden agitation as she had, descending from the fell, and then to pause to find out what it was he wanted to do to her now. She was game for anything.

He was curious about all of her, every single part of her, just as she was about him, and she wanted him to be that way, but they didn't have that much time.

He stayed back, as she ran the bath for him… for them both, he hoped, then went off to dig out clothing, also for them both, returning in minutes to check the water.

She took him into her arms again and encouraged him into the bath, where she began to wash him with soap and a sponge. This way, she would cover every square inch of his body, which she would never have been able to do if her mother had not gone out.

Had her mother stayed, she would have had to have run his bath, get it ready for him, sort some clothes out, and then leave him to see to himself. That wouldn't have been fair on either him, or her. They'd both needed to do it this way.

She encouraged him to sit down so she could reach over and do his hair as he reached up to her to touch under her breasts, holding them as she leaned over him. He held them still with his hand, as she vigorously worked on his head. He moved to touch, from one to the other, always fascinated by them.

He began to revive again, but he'd never fully gone away.

She moved some of the shampoo down on him there, smoothing the soap along him, getting him excited again in preparation for what would happen next.

He gripped her arm, lifted and pulled her, with a gentle cry from her, over onto him, bringing her into the bath with him as he took over from her, washing her in turn as she sat between his legs.

It was his turn to learn about her now—and he did—doing to her, what she had done to him, but being careful not to wet her hair.

After those preliminaries, they each became more focused again.

He moved her to be under him, went between her legs and held himself there, letting her see what he had planned for her as he looked into her face, asking permission.

She laughed and pulled him down to kiss her, feeling him find her, and slide into her. That was spectacularly easy, this time.

He was like a human dynamo. How had she got so lucky?

Water sloshed everywhere as they writhed together.

He felt as though he was even deeper into her than ever before, but the water had helped smooth the way.

Then, everything subsided once more.

They were both out of breath this time.

He laughed as he kissed her hungrily, still pushing to let her know where he was… as if she didn't know exactly where he was. "When I come out of you, we will have no choice but to get out of here quickly, my love."

He was getting into the swing of it now.

He explained. "Sperm does not behave well in water, and sticks to everything; skin, hair, and it's awkward to find and deal with, but we can stay like this for a while anyway, as long as we don't move too much."

She laughed. "We can't stay for too long. I still have to see that my brother's clothes fit you, get myself dressed, see to dinner, clean this mess up, wash around the bath, and set the table."

He could help. He wasn't helpless.

"I've been house-trained. I can set the table. You just tell me where the things are."

He moved up the bath with her, and somehow, swung them both out of the bath without leaving her body and carried her across to the toilet.

She sat there, getting rid of him into the toilet bowl as he dried around her and all over her as he stood in front of her for her to admire and to learn.

She took over and dried him then, as he stood above her.

They were running out of time.

He helped her tidy up and to wipe down the bath, making sure they left no sign of what they had done.

By the time they were dressed and went downstairs, they both had to co-operate, to be finished before the others got back.

She'd looked good in shorts. She looked even better in a dress. He wanted to interfere, but knew that he shouldn't.

She told him where everything was, and he set the table according to her instructions as she checked the dinner and the potatoes.

Not a moment too soon.

They'd just got everything done, when her family arrived, making enough noise.

Mrs. Prescott had obviously told her husband and sons, something of what would greet them; what their sister had 'dragged' off the fell this time. Telling them to be well mannered toward him and to watch what they said.

They all trooped in, getting rid of their damp clothes in the porch and waited for introductions as they sized up this… whatever, whoever he was.

Why was Louise in a dress? She wore shorts all summer.

They'd read between the lines of what their mother had told them about him.

And this was the sod that was knocking off their sister and trying to look like butter wouldn't melt in his mouth. They didn't say what they were thinking. They rarely did.

Their mother took over.

"No, no, we don't need to go through all these pointless introductions. We can get those out of the way later, after dinner.

"You'll be staying the night." She was looking at James as she said that.

She wasn't going to argue about that, and nor was he. It was obvious that wild horses wouldn't have dragged him away from Louise without a fight, and vice versa. Wherever he went, Louise would be going with him, so best not to open that can of worms.

It was startling for a mother to see that.

"I wouldn't send a dog out on a night like this."

He might be rising in the world. Toad… snake… dog.

She intended to grill him; sit him under bright lights and give him the third degree as she asked questions about him and her daughter; bringing out the apocryphal sock, full of wet sand, to soften him up a bit.

"Besides, I want to know how you two met on the fell, and how you managed to get her dry before you brought her home."

It was beginning already! Yes, she would want to know that.

Tricky questions. She'd better not ask how they'd managed to get her dressed in his clothes, and him, in some of hers.

Or had Louise been the moving force in all of it, ensnaring him and bringing him home with her and giving him no choice in the matter?

Could they have met somewhere else, some other time, and they'd plotted it this way?

"Sit down, start on the bread rolls. Louise and I will serve everything."

The men sat quietly and waited. The questions could come, later.

James wasn't fooled. They were sizing him up. The atmosphere was not friendly. He could even taste it.

So, this man was molesting their sister and daughter! Let's de-bag him and take him out behind the barn and beat the crap out of him!

Her daughter looked flustered and flushed, as she waited on the men, but she was also bright eyed, ready to leap to James's defense if her brothers decided to be pushy, or if her father began to question him too closely. Her mother, too.

If they weren't careful, they would wind up with hot gravy in their laps.

James looked relaxed and ready for anything, sitting back and staying silent.

Mrs. Prescott saw everything. The silence often said more than the words. He'd expected this kind of reception from her defensive family. All would-be-suitors did, at first… and sometimes afterward… if he didn't fit. He wanted to fit. They would have to let him in for the sake of their sister and daughter.

Louise was tense, but he wasn't, and he had a stubborn set to his jaw, and a look in his eyes that said, *'be careful if you mess with me or with this woman that I love and that is now mine'.*

What was truly surprising was that he seemed to fit in to the family group already. That, was the truly disturbing part of it.

He was proving to be much more than first met the eye, and he was in love with Louise already. They were both in love.

If she and her family did not handle this cautiously, she knew, beyond any doubt, that they would antagonize her daughter and him beyond any chance of recovery, and lose them both.

How did one deal with this?

Her daughter probably didn't know what she'd bitten into with this man, but…. There was always a, 'but'.

She more than likely did know, and that was why she'd brought him home, into this lion's den, and had let him get into her panties in record time. Louise had only been gone about eight hours, but those hours had changed her life in every way.

That thought about him having been with her daughter, 'that' way (she should never have gone out to pick up her husband and sons, except the 'worst' had already happened before Louise had got home), had her wanting to tear her hair out, feeling so helpless for once, and it had happened like a flash of lightning, upsetting their staid little family.

That pair had been up to something while she'd been out, and it didn't take more than one guess to decide what that had been. Still, they hadn't had much time for … except they'd had more than enough time. Not that it made any difference, or lessened the crime.

Their clothes had been washed and dried too, when they should have waited until after his bath. And how had she done that? There wasn't enough hot water for a wash and for both of them to get a bath, and yet... they'd... both... bathed.

She thought about that. Hellfire! They'd been in the bath together! She felt as though her legs wouldn't support her. The nerve of it! If she was right.

That thought took her back a few years.

She was distracted for just a second as her eyes flashed to her daughter, seeing her blushing, and the cornered look in her eyes as she'd looked back at her, knowing exactly what her mother had been thinking, knowing.

Her mother knew everything that had happened!

James managed to intervene to stop Mrs. Prescott from dropping the heavy platter of meat onto the table and breaking things. He'd moved fast to do that, but he'd been closer than anyone else.

She watched him put it down in the cleared space on the table. It would have been hot on his hands, but he said nothing.

"Thank you."

Whatever they'd done, was done. There was nothing she could do about it now, so she couldn't criticize anything, but she'd have a lot to say to Louise, later. They'd been a busy pair with bathing, dressing, that wash, as well as looking after dinner. How had they found time for anything else?

Then she remembered when she'd been courting. She and Mr. Prescott had managed a lot of impossible things. It was surprising what one could do in even ten minutes of being left alone when one was determined, and desperately horny. She'd even got pregnant with Trevor one of those times.

The men were altogether too quiet, sizing this stranger up as they passed things around the table, wondering how their sister had met him, and why she'd dragged him home the way she had.

She'd never brought any boys or men home before.

Who was he, really? What was he?

He didn't smile much except at their sister. When he met their eyes, he held them. He even smiled.

Mrs. Prescott knew that smile. She'd seen it on her husband's face once, when someone had been taunting him as they'd both finished high school. It was a fixed kind of smile, frozen on her boyfriend's face. The next thing she knew was that the tormentor was flat on his back with a bloody nose.

Did James feel that threatened by them?

Yes, he did.

She hoped she didn't have to intervene. She would have to do some delicate, or not so delicate, distracting. She took a deep breath. Her heart was beating too fast.

"You can say grace, Louise."

An explosive confession.

They sat forward with their heads bowed as their daughter gave thanks.

Mrs. Prescott studied her daughter. She was holding James's hand under the table. He was still smiling. Louise didn't look any different. She didn't seem distressed or guilty in any way, as a girl often did when a man went at her for the first, traumatic time. Maybe what she was thinking, was wrong.

"Lord…. Bless this food for our use. And keep this company safe from all harm. Let their thoughts not be troubled, and please keep peace within, and outside of the family."

Not, 'our thoughts' but, 'their thoughts'.

And then she threw the cat in with the pigeons.

"And thank you, Lord, for bringing James, my fiancé, to me today on the Fell as he helped me, and probably saved my life by what he did. Amen."

Her fiancé?

Louise sat back, looking at no one, and she waited.

There was a deathly silence around the table. The only things to be heard for a few seconds were the sizzling of the kettle and the ticking of the clock.

Someone chuckled.

Mr. Prescott! *He* knew what was going on.

"Pass the meat will you, please?"

They all dived into the food despite what they'd heard. They had their priorities right. *Eat first. Fight, later.* Some things should not be done on an empty stomach.

Not much would hold hungry men back. The questions would fly later. No one was going anywhere in this weather.

Her daughter hadn't said anything to her like that, to warn her before she'd left the house just over an hour earlier. They can't have wrapped it up so shockingly neatly in just the time she'd been out. They hadn't had time to talk that much, but maybe they had, while they'd been on that Fell. A lot of things had happened up there. As well as happening down here, as they'd got that other, constantly demanding presence and urgent need they both had, out of the way.

It had come as a shock to them all, but the questions would wait.

Perhaps it was a shock to James, too. If so, it was not an unwelcome shock. Never had there been such drama around the table. She'd half expected that Trevor, the elder of her boys would have been the first, explaining why he and the neighbor's daughter he'd grown up with, just had to get married fast, and it would soon have to be faster, with Marj being almost two months 'gone', already.

Except, Louise had just beaten him to it. She'd stolen his thunder in a decisive way.

James had his hand on their daughter's bare leg under the edge of the table, and of her dress, to comfort her, or to encourage her, and he was smiling at her, shocked by her courage. It seemed as much of a shock to him, as it had been to all of them. He leaned over and whispered something to Louise that only she could hear.

The look she gave him back, told them everything. Gratitude. Love!

They were in love and they knew all about each other in every sense of that, 'know', word.

They'd shared that bath and everything that went with it! They'd be sharing a bed tonight, too, regardless of what anyone might think, or say.

There was nothing anyone could do about it.

"That was quite an admission to throw at us like that. So, how long have you two been engaged, James? It's the first we've heard of it." Mr. Prescott just had to know. He was looking at James, waiting.

James was flustered for a moment. He had not clearly understood the question. 'Engaged' meant different things to him at this moment. He'd certainly been engaged with their daughter in an intimate way, but her father wasn't asking about that specific activity, but about that other meaning of that word.

James recovered, and answered as he looked at the clock.

"About six hours." It was also not far off when he and Louise had also first been 'engaged' in that other way.

They can't have discussed it, or touched on it anywhere in any detail, but it was so unthinkable, it had to be true.

And then a more pointed question. "And when was it you first met, and presumably fell in love with my daughter?" They must have met somewhere else, before now, to be so…relaxed… the way they were with each other.

James looked pained to have to admit it, so soon after that first admission.

"About six hours ago too. And a couple of minutes." He was answering both meanings of that word. He'd tell Louise about the alternative meanings later and give her a laugh too.

Her brothers both laughed nervously at the preposterousness of that explanation, but their giggling was soon cut short.

They wouldn't ask the other questions burning the air, about what he'd done to their sister to have so screwed her up, as well as screwing her. It was too obvious.

Their sister! She didn't look any different. Though there was that dress. It suited her too.

She'd said something about him 'probably' saving her life…. That must have been 'theatrics', to give the family something else to talk about… to throw them off the more pointed questions? It was also doubtful.

But he'd obviously got into her panties out on the fell in that rain if he hadn't got them entirely off her—the devious sod—and she'd, just as obviously, let him shag her (they could imagine it happening), or he'd be missing an eye and his balls, and he'd still be out there.

Who would have believed it…? Their uptight, prude of a sister, and he'd knocked her off; was still, figuratively and literally, knocking her off. So, which of them had been the first to get that particular ball, rolling?

They didn't need to ask.

Their sister had started this. A man would never have dared to make that first move for fear of being accused of rape, and she'd never have wanted to bring him home to face this.

They almost felt sorry for him.

When their sister made up her mind....

They began to see their quiet sister through different eyes. And they thought they'd had nothing to learn from her?

It looked like they were losing the urge to lunge at this strange man over the table. He was an utterly unknown quantity; someone to be envied.

Their plates were loaded anyway, and the table was full.

He'd caught them off guard as much as Louise had, choosing her moment well-- when everyone was sitting down-- and after pleading for their thoughts not to be troubled, and for peace.

Nice touch, that.

They didn't know what to make of him, or even if they could believe either of them.

Except they could be believed. They were both too calm and sure about themselves.

"Enough!"

Mrs. Prescott raised her voice and brought the flat of her down on the table, hard, setting the cutlery dancing, bringing them all back to ground. She was staring at Trevor and David, her sons, both of whom looked gobsmacked.

Her husband wasn't likely to make too much of a fuss, but like her, he'd want to know a lot of things.

"We eat, first."

The lynching can come later.

She laughed as she looked around the table.

"And I thought Trevor would be the first to shock us." She had to get that off her chest. *She,* knew how to choose her moment, too.

Trevor?

He looked lost. How had the conversation turned back to him so fast? What did they know? He was sitting there, blushing.

Oh shit! It looked like absolutely everyone knew.

Their mother added another piece of the puzzle. "With Marjorie Butler." She hadn't needed to add that. Who else would it have been? They'd gone once too often—in all of the many hundreds of times they'd been known to have been intimate—to that particular well.

Trevor was close to panicking now. His sister was shaking her head at him. How had he landed in this shit when his sister was the one…?

She hadn't told on him, but she'd known about Marjorie. So, who'd told?

Marj had a gabby, much younger sister… too many sisters who were difficult to keep track of, and who'd seen too much that one time. Many times, when they had been babysitting. It had to have been one of her sisters.

Louise was proving to be a woman to be reckoned with. She was also friends with Marjorie, so she'd known about what they'd been doing to each other for a long time, and she'd kept their secret while warning him what would happen, dropping hints about 'little pitchers….' She'd been right.

Let he who is without guilt….

"We'll talk about all of this, later. And we'll keep it polite."

Mrs. Prescott's word was law.

She'd just defused one problem by raising another.

The heat was dying down for James. Louise thanked her mother with her eyes.

"Eat. We didn't go to all this trouble for it to get cold, or go to waste."

Everything became deathly silent and painfully polite after that as they ate, and far too politely asking someone to pass this, that, or the other, as the questions faded and were stored away until later.

David was the only one left with any sense of the ridiculous and to be able to move beyond the obvious tension.

"Trevor, dear, bent, older brother, may I politely request that you politely parse me the polite potatoes, pretty please and thank you?"

He got an elbow in his ribs for that. Trevor was not amused.

"Now, boys."

His father glared at David, just out of reach under the table or he would have kicked him, but at least the ice had been broken.

Wrapping things up.

After they'd made a good start on dinner, it was Mrs. Prescott who began the conversation, deciding that it was safe again. She would be the only one saying anything.

"So, when did you two plan on telling us, properly?" Her question was directed at Louise and James. She'd get to Trevor after that if he was unwise enough to be still here.

"And I expect you even know exactly when the wedding will be?"

It would be soon, but not for Trevor's reason. Not after just six hours together, although they must have been very busy… that way.

They needed to be slowed down. Except, nothing would slow them down now.

There was not a hint of hesitation or any sign of being embarrassed, in her daughter's response.

"We don't know, Mom. We haven't planned that far yet. We did only just meet (at least she had the grace to blush), but we should marry as soon as reasonably possible."

James had nothing to say. Those two would talk about it tonight.

"I'll be going to live in Manchester when I start my job at the high school in another two weeks. James is already living near my school as he finishes at the university, and we thought that we should share, somewhere."

Her brothers' eyes flew from one to the other, not believing what they were hearing.

Holy hell! Was this their sister?

"We haven't discussed it in detail yet, but we know we will be living together." That seemed to be understood already.

James never said a word, just taking it all in and passing things to others before they were asked for.

When her daughter came out of her shell, she shocked even her brothers, and nothing, but nothing, would ever usually shock them.

The more they listened to Louise explain how things would be, the more the tension had dropped. It was a done deal.

Their sister was clearly happy with what was happening to her, and she was very much in charge. They could learn something from her.

They took another, closer look at this strangely silent young man again.

He looked to be a not-too-bad kind of a guy, albeit with a knowing smile on his face, while remaining silent, letting Louise do all of the talking. Wise man.

He seemed to have a good appetite and a cast iron digestive system not to have been put off dinner by their focused animosity and the obviously shocking revelations. This… unknown… was an observer and a thinker. He also ate like he hadn't eaten for a week—like most, vigorously healthy (and horny) young men— but Mrs. Prescott knew that Mrs. Abernethy fed her guests well, and she always made up a mountain of a packed lunch for them.

"You can tell us about your plans later, Dear. Before we retire." She had to try and slow things down. She looked at her husband and boys.

"So, how did your days go at work?"

Nothing like their sister's hectic day, that was sure!

Her husband ignored the question. He found his daughter's untold... but obvious... story, to be more amusing than revolutionary. He'd half expected something like this would happen to liven the family up, sooner or later.

"What do you do at university James?"

Get him talking.

"I'm in, math. At Manchester." All eyes were on him now. "I just finished my first degree, as Louise did, and am working on my thesis. I'll be another two or three years getting that out of the way, and I'm also teaching at a local high school too." He wouldn't dare tell them the title of his thesis. They might throw things at him.

"So, you met there; at the university."

"No, sir. We never met at university. We first met a few hours ago."

He'd already told them that, but it hadn't seemed believable.

"Let the poor man eat, Harold. He's starving, and he's been out on the Fell all day. He got soaked getting Louise home safely."

He'd been soaking wet when she'd first seen him, but he hadn't seemed to be in any way 'distressed'. How 'safe' her daughter had been at any time in his company was also debatable, considering that he'd seemed to be… that way… 'stemmy', with her daughter hanging close to him, trying to hide that condition from her mother. He hadn't got that way by accident. He'd had help!

After dinner was completed, James thanked Mrs. Prescott for her hospitality, and for the dinner, and for seeing that he was dressed in dry clothes. Even if Louise had done that for him… eventually… probably after a lot of negotiating that she would always be on the losing… or winning end of.

At least he wasn't lacking in manners.

About now was when the real questions would begin, except they were all required to help tidy their plates away and help with the washing up.

After that, both boys excused themselves. They didn't need to stay for coffee, or desert… or risk them being dragged deeper into this, especially not Trevor. One shock for him, was enough.

It was a done deal between the two of them. Their sister wasn't complaining about what he'd obviously done to her, and would continue to do every chance he got, so why should they? They had other plans for their Friday evening, which involved doing that same thing too, to one of their sister's willing friends.

Trevor had to go and talk to Marj's parents to get that outstanding difficulty out of the way with the least possible embarrassment, and David had a dance to go to0.

Marj would find some way to make sure Trevor stayed the night with her, even if he had to climb back in through her bedroom window.

Knowing when to Accept the Inevitable.

After the house had settled down, the four remaining adults sat around the table.

Mr. Prescott began.

"What's going on here, Louise?" Straight to the point.

"What happened today out there? I know this new job has been on your mind a lot recently."

He looked at James.

"Or maybe I should ask you."

Louise laid her hand over James's. She would deal with this.

"No, Dad. It's for me to say something."

They waited for her to begin.

"I did have a lot on my mind when I went out this morning."

She got her thoughts in order, deciding how much to say.

"I was beginning to feel overwhelmed with changes in my life." She toyed with the cutlery. "I was going to be leaving home, getting my first real job, and I needed to find somewhere to live, close to that job. Mostly, I think I was feeling depressed about leaving home, even though I'd already been three years away at university, but that was more like… school. This break, seemed more final."

"So, what happened, dear?" Mrs. Prescott joined in.

"I needed to think, so I went for a walk across the fell as I usually do. I was so engrossed, I missed the signs of the weather until I woke up to how hard it was raining all of a sudden, and then I was startled by the lightning and heard the thunder. I'd never seen a downpour like that. By then I was too wet for my own good, so I took shelter as much as I could, up near 'Round Knot', 'till it blew over, but it didn't."

She was re-living that.

"I was depressed, wet, and cold. I even prayed for things to change." She wouldn't say anything about crying in her frustration; but she had.

"The next thing I knew, there was a man standing there in front of me, speaking to me.

"This man." She looked at James.

Her parents knew that look.

"It was as though a guardian angel had found me. I thought my prayers had been answered, and then I discovered that they really had been."

She wondered how much she dared to say.

"He sheltered me under that Poncho-- hanging just outside the door-- to get me warm and even drier than I was. You should take a look at it… it opens up…."

They didn't want to hear about a poncho.

"We sheltered together under that. We talked for hours… waiting for the storm to pass, or the rain to let up, but it didn't."

She took a deep breath and blurted out her feelings.

"As we talked, I fell in love with him, Mom, in those first moments. I never expected it, and not out there. We both fell in love, and we both knew it. I felt as though I knew all about him in the first few minutes."

She went over in her mind, how it had developed between them as he'd gradually undressed her, striving to protect her modesty at the same time, waiting for her to object. She was too cold and wet to object. And it had gradually run away from them both after that, but she couldn't tell her parents about any of that.

James was smiling, touching her leg under the table, wondering how much she would dare say before her father decided to attack him.

She blushed as she told what she could, her glance going from one parent to the other as they listened patiently.

"Don't ask me to explain, because I'm not sure that I can. All I know is that I never want to be separated from this man again, and I won't be."

She was throwing down the gauntlet.

"He changed my life, totally. I can't understand how it happened so fast, how everything I didn't even know I wanted, was right there with me." …for the taking, if she'd had the courage. She'd found the courage, rather than risk losing him.

"He rescued me, got me off the fell, with that rain still coming down, and… you know the rest."

Like hell they did, but some things were best not enquired about.

"You said, he saved your life. Were you that wet and cold?"

She nodded. "I was soaked through. I would have been hard pressed to get home the way I was, so… maybe it wasn't so melodramatic, but I'm glad I didn't have to find out." So were they.

She was missing out too much. She'd glossed over several hours with a few sentences. There were holes in her narrative big enough to drive a bus through, but they could imagine… all too easily.

He'd got most of her clothes off her, and given her some of his.

And what else had he given her? Unfortunately, it didn't take a Rhodes scholar to figure that one out.

"We want to get married, and soon, Dad. In the next holiday before Christmas, about six weeks away." She looked from her mother to her father, waiting for them to object; to say something. No one seemed ready to object. Not even James.

"I don't care what anyone says or how sudden it is. I want it understood, and before he leaves here on Sunday." They understood that ultimatum.

"James goes back to Manchester on the Sunday evening train. I've decided that I'll be packed by then as well, and that I'll be going with him."

There was no objection. How could they safely object? They waited for her to continue. James didn't even object.

"I know where I will be living when I start that job. James told me something of the older couple he lives with. You can visit anytime, but we'll be back here, or visiting his family on most weekends."

No one seemed to be objecting.

"What about you, James? Do your parents know about this?" Mrs. Prescott answered her own question. "No, you haven't had time."

"I'll phone them tonight and let them know, or I'll do it tomorrow. They'll meet us off the train in Manchester. They live not so far away. We'll phone you when we get in."

He seemed considerate that way, but why wouldn't he be? Everything a young man might ever want had just dropped into his lap on that Fell.

Did he know what kind of a treasure he'd found?

"We'll have to meet them too."

They weren't arguing against any of this?

Everything seemed to be a fait accompli. No argument. No fighting over it.

However, there would still be a lot of questions, and a lot more details to fill in before they would feel comfortable with this, if they ever could, until after the actual marriage.

Mrs. Prescott hadn't asked about them swapping clothing yet, or about them bathing together. She must know about that, and it must be eating at her to know.

Her father still had a comment. "You two got everything wrapped up before you even got here. If you're sure about all of this?" It had happened blindingly fast.

He hadn't needed to ask.

They were sure, and there was nothing that anyone with a lick of sense would try to do about it to change it, without creating a major disruption in too many lives, including their own.

"Break out that bottle of Port, Harold. We'll toast this pair and then take ourselves off to bed. We have an early start in the morning. There's a big shop to do."

Mrs. Prescott excused herself, going through to the distant parlor before bringing a small box back with her.

She opened it and took out a small cloth bag containing various rings.

"These rings are my mother's and father's. They are so crippled with arthritis and swollen joints that they can no longer wear them. Rather than see them lost, they gave them to me. They are her engagement ring and both of their wedding rings. They wanted you to have them." She was looking at her daughter. "Wear them, if you like. They may help stave off some awkward questions until you replace them." When they got married.

“We’ll bid you two, goodnight. One down, Harold. Two, to go.”

With that, they were gone, leaving the two of them alone.

No one would ask about sleeping arrangements. That was for them to sort out for themselves.

Fait Accompli.

Both Louise and James seemed dazed by the turn of events for the better, when they couldn't have been sure it would have gone so easily their way.

James moved around to sit at the head of the table where he could hold Louise's hands as he looked at her.

He leaned over and kissed her, then kissed her hands. "You succeeded." He sounded surprised.

"We, succeeded, James."

He picked up the rings from the table.

"There's something else we should do before we retire."

Her eyes sparkled, not sure what he would suggest. It wasn't that private where they were, and it would take her parents a few minutes to settle… if they could ever settle after that shock. She waited to hear what he would ask.

"We've done everything so far, in reverse order, except for learning each other's names."

He lowered his voice as he looked at her, kissing her fingers.

"After a tricky start… for me… we mostly undressed each other in the first few minutes." He still couldn't believe how that had gone.

"I'm not sure you were aware of how excited for you I was, even then."

She knew. She had felt him beneath her, and had seen the changes in his expression… becoming more flustered and flushed, as he'd progressively undressed her.

She'd even let him. Then, she'd broken out of her shell even more, and had decided that they must make love.

"And then we were intimate… almost in the first hour. It was something I could never have expected in a hundred years. I still can't believe it. There was no going back for us, after that.

"I shall thank you for the rest of my life for being able to take that first step, and for getting it out of the way between us. We only seemed to 'grow' from there."

She liked to hear him describe what he'd felt and experienced. At least he hadn't been so shocked as to want nothing to do with her, after her total abandonment of moral values. She still had more than enough morals, but of a different kind.

"After all that we had learned, I was never so excited as when I was getting you dressed again to come home (she'd known all about that; had felt it for herself... after all, he had been inside of her, and as hard as blazes while he'd been doing that), and it only seemed to get better and better."

It had for her, too.

"When you dropped that bombshell on everyone at dinner, about us being engaged, I almost died."

He'd hidden it well. Except for his hand, tightening on her leg.

"I half expected to be attacked right there and then by the entire family, but they didn't, despite it being so obvious what we'd done to each other to get that far so soon."

He knew the firm ground he was upon now, so could open up, himself, even more, and put the proper finishing touches to this.

"I suppose it's only right that I complete this circle, and ask you to marry me—which should have been the first thing—but that was out of the question at that moment. We'd only just met. But look what we did instead! I suppose we had to mix things up in order to move forward as we did."

She waited to see what else he would say.

"I have one other thing to ask of you, my love."

"What?"

"Please be careful what you tell my sisters about this, or they'll come looking for me in the wrong kind of way."

"I'll be careful."

"No. I meant that you should tell them *everything*. It's the only way they'll believe you, and the only way I'll be able to survive."

She smiled at him.

"Are you sure that you really want to marry me, James, after I gave in so easily to you?"

"What about me? Why would you want to marry me, after I couldn't help myself about what happened, and took such cruel advantage of you? I had no self-control whatsoever."

She obviously forgave him.

"It's nice that you still want to marry me, James. considering how fast everything else took place between us, I was almost beginning to think you'd never ask." She'd thought nothing of the kind. "What took you so long?"

They both laughed. She knew it was what they both wanted.

He slid the engagement ring on her finger.

"Now. Let's do this properly between us, shall we? Two more steps to go, my love."

"Two? But James (she still was able to blush), we can't undress completely. Not down here. We could be interrupted. Mom will be restless for a while."

"Not that step just yet, my love. But soon. That's the second step, not the first one, and we will be private for that one."

He patted his knee. "You should come and sit over here with me, on my lap, as we complete this."

She did so, not sure what he intended, putting her arms around him.

"We need to be physically close for this. It would not do for us to wake your parents up. It will not be a legal marriage ceremony, although, in the old days, it was all that a couple needed to do to be married, and I think it will make us both feel better." He kissed her.

He was feeling better already, and was even becoming frisky too, as she could feel, the way his hand slid up her dress.

He'd checked that she still had panties on.

"We'll make our own vows, here and now, to each other, and then we can justifiably, maybe, wear these wedding rings, and hold our heads high."

"Then, James, we can consummate our union." She wanted to do that too, feeling his excitement beneath her.

"Yes, my eager love. We can."

She seemed to like that suggestion.

After a little thought, they looked each other in the eyes, and said what was closest to their hearts concerning each other. They'd try to remember what they said later, and make sure those vows were written down and recorded for their children to read.

"It once was legal enough, and it will do until we can do it legally."

They kissed, binding them into that contract with each other.

Louise rested her head on his shoulder. She felt like crying again. This time, with happiness. "James?"

"Hm. hm." He was kissing her on the neck.

"We still could…down here... if you want to."

He perked up. "How?"

"Move your chair back a little. This dress will hide a lot. If you don't mind teasing my panties off, I'll sit on you again, and you can… you know."

He knew.

It took about five seconds to move his hand under her dress and to tease her panties off as she helped get him free again, for her to sit upon him and for him to move into her as she faced him to kiss him, straddling over him, feeling him going slowly into her.

They were both on fire almost immediately, presaging a busy evening together.

Once they'd both come down from that high, he pushed her panties up into her between her legs to catch what he'd left her with, covered himself away, and moved over to the stairs with her as she led him there. They would continue this upstairs.

He seemed to hesitate. "I'm not sure what your mother will accept so soon under her roof. She brought some bedding out onto the settee."

"That's not for you. It's for David, or Trevor. They won't get back until late anyway—especially Trevor. They know they shouldn't upset the house with their stumbling around. The Butlers are a family of five girls, and they all dote on him, so he'll be a prisoner over there, maybe for a day or two, explaining himself… among other things.

"They'll likely get married before we will, maybe even next weekend. Mom will let me know.

"You are going to be with me, in my bedroom, and you will be doing to me, for the rest of the night, what we will be doing to each other for the rest of our lives. You are going to sleep with me, in my arms as you also hold me close, kissing me, and making love to me whenever we awake. I'll change the bedding on Sunday morning and get it into the wash before we leave."

He protested, but only weakly. "They'll object to that happening so soon after we met, and us not married. They don't know me. They can't possibly trust me that soon."

"They trust my judgment. Besides, we are now unofficially married. We said our vows. And we just did that other, too."

She clenched her legs tighter on her panties. There'd be a lot of that from him over the next days, weeks, months, years.

"There's only one thing to be careful about. I'd better not get pregnant. I'll tell the school I'm getting married soon, in case things don't go as I intend, and we do make a mistake. I'll let them know that I will be using my maiden name. Miss Prescott, unless they decide otherwise." He was not resisting now.

"C'mon. Let's go to bed, James. If we get up early in the morning, we can go in with Mom and Dad. They still have a thousand questions to ask, and so do I."

She led him to the stairs.